DEAD VELVET CHEESECAKE
A Southern Psychic Sisters Mystery

A. GARDNER

D1738594

For Ebby

Dear Ms. Ember Greene,

Due to a lack of available Seers, you have been assigned to case WGH-11 in Cottonberry, Alabama. We trust you will find a peaceful solution to this sensitive matter.

Kind regards,
The Clairs

Chapter 1

"This is a bakery, not a nude beach."

Mary Jean added eggs to her cream-cheese mixture one at a time and slowly adjusted her stance. She wore multiple layers underneath her dusty pink knit sweater. It was a stark contrast to her fellow classmate Cindy's spaghetti-strap top with a plunging neckline. I wondered how Mary Jean handled the humidity with all of that fabric draped over her torso.

"Yes, I know," Cindy replied, lifting her chin and checking the consistency of her cheesecake batter. "You told me that last week."

"Y'all should really think about enforcing a dress code," Mary Jean continued. "Young Kalen over there is only eighteen years old. No sweet and innocent boy should have to see all that." Her eyes shifted to the other end of the kitchen where Cindy was placing her cheesecake in the oven.

"I really don't mind." Kalen raised his eyebrows and touched the rim of his thick-framed glasses as he watched Cindy from his seat at the counter.

Rickiah, Zinny, and Darlene giggled as they uncovered the red velvet cake layers they'd made the previous week.

This was my sister Stevie's second time teaching, and already she was about to lose it. She clenched her jaw as she observed her students—a tester class of six Misty Key locals to perfect her curriculum before offering her baking course to the public. The bakery had been overwhelmed with interest, and Stevie had come up with a series of classes to teach anyone the basics of baking. She'd even created special cakes and desserts to complete as take-home projects during each class. It was a great way to add additional income to the family business, but Stevie was proving to be less patient with her customers than I'd expected.

"Mary Jean, if you spent less time worrying about everyone else, you wouldn't be so behind," Stevie said through her teeth.

I stepped in before she ran out of things to say in place of swear words.

"That would be a good suggestion to write on your customer survey," I said. "You'll receive one at the end of the course." I glanced at Stevie and nodded. She took a deep breath.

"OK, let's get our red velvet cake layers ready for the cheesecake filling." Stevie stood firm at the head of the kitchen. "Watch how I trim the top of my cakes to make them level."

Kalen raised his hand. "Have you ever added butter to your cheesecakes?" He narrowed his eyes as he watched Stevie's demonstration.

"Yes, Kalen," she answered. "Like I told you earlier, it depends on the type of cheesecake you're making."

"What about flavored butters?" His tall, lanky frame leaned against the counter.

"You ask a lot of questions," Stevie said.

"His girlfriend will be pleased," Cindy chimed in from across the room. She winked in Kalen's direction, and a twisted smile crossed his face. Cindy Buford was my mother's secret nemesis from the Misty Key Women's Society. She was in her fifties, yet she dressed like a college freshman. She'd also been married six times. She'd signed up for the class to improve her cooking skills. At least, that's what she'd said her first day in the kitchen.

"I don't know how you have time for a girlfriend." Rickiah Pepper, a dear family friend, chuckled as she followed Stevie's lead and cut the top of her red velvet cakes. "With everything going on at the Crystal Grande Hotel since Mr. Carmichael came back from the dead, I'm surprised you have any time off, Kalen."

"He was lost at sea," Zinny pointed out. "Unless you have a different theory?" She studied Rickiah carefully and scratched the side of her wrinkled cheek. Zinny had been the least interested in baking, and Stevie was convinced she'd only enrolled in the course to gather more gossip for her column at the *Misty Messenger*.

"Are you planning on making anything today, Zinny?" Stevie placed her hands on her hips.

"My cheesecake is in the oven just like everybody else's." She pointed across the kitchen and flipped a piece of wavy, gray hair over her shoulder.

"Don't even think about coming around my shop tonight for a piece," Darlene added as she stepped back to admire her skills. "This baby is a special treat just for Harold and me."

I was relieved when Darlene Johnston, owner of the antiques shop down the street, had signed up for Stevie's course. I knew Stevie would need as many mellow personalities as she could get until she'd gotten used to the idea of teaching. Not to mention the course was perfect for Darlene, who planned on using her new skills to create birthday cakes for her seventeen grandkids.

"I don't suppose you have any fresh insights on the return of George Carmichael, do you, boy?" Zinny left her sunken cakes untouched and looked at Kalen.

"I just park cars," he answered.

"You must hear things." She watched him set his red velvet cakes on top of each other and take a picture. He was on his phone more than my little sister, Aqua.

"All people are talking about these days is that big party the Carmichael twins are throwing," he responded, staying focused on his cake.

"Ugh, Mardi Gras," Mary Jean muttered. "I don't know why anyone in this town participates in such sinful celebrations."

"Come on, Mary Jean. We do it every February." Rickiah smiled, trying to push away the storm cloud Mary Jean seemed to drag around wherever she went. "The parties. The parades. The food. You might actually have fun."

"Heaven forbid," Cindy quietly added. She let out a soft giggle.

"I want her out of here." Mary Jean pointed at Cindy and glared in her direction.

Stevie continued to take deep breaths as she reached for her cooled layer of cheesecake filling.

This was the reason I'd decided to attend every class.

"It doesn't work that way, Mary Jean." I approached the subject as casually as possible.

"I'm not paying to be ridiculed." She stamped her foot.

"If you're unhappy with anything, please leave a comment on your customer survey," I replied. "Each of you will receive that survey at the end of the course."

"Got it." Rickiah displayed a thumbs-up for everyone to see.

Mary Jean rolled her eyes and got back to leveling her cakes.

"Poor Mrs. Carmichael," Darlene continued. "I can't imagine how she must be feeling. Her husband declared dead all those years. I hear he made a huge fuss at the hotel when he found out about the remodel. He fired that Indie Wilkes fella and everything."

I automatically wrinkled my nose at the mention of the hotel's ex-manager and Mrs. Carmichael's former business partner. My first encounter with him had been short and not-so-sweet. My second meeting with him had consisted of him calling the police and trying to cancel the town's annual craft fair. His temper was just as short as he was. I knew I wasn't the only one in Misty Key who had been happy to see him and his awful khaki suits go when George Carmichael resurfaced.

"That's interesting," Zinny responded. "Hold that thought, Darlene, until I get back from the restroom."

"You sure do take a lot of bathroom breaks," Cindy commented.

Zinny walked out of the kitchen and into the café to use the bathroom.

"Remember, no smoking," I shouted after her.

The rest of the evening sped by as Stevie showed everyone how to assemble the layers of her red velvet cheesecake. She proceeded to frost it and walk around the room helping anyone who needed guidance. The conversation centered around the Carmichaels' extravagant Mardi Gras festivities, with Mary Jean muttering comments about how Mardi Gras was the devil's holiday.

When the class came to an end, I counted all of our equipment and helped the students box up their weekly creations to take home. Cindy left first, as she usually did. Kalen, who was running late for work, followed, and then Darlene. Mary Jean was last to finish her cheesecake, and she rushed outside tailed by Zinny, who was dead set on asking her more questions about her thoughts on Mardi Gras and the Crystal Grande Hotel.

I helped Stevie wipe the counters.

"I shouldn't be sweating this much." Stevie stopped for a moment and wiped her forehead. She tugged at her long-sleeved shirt, which she'd worn to cover the sleeve of tattoos on her forearm. "But you were right about covering my tattoos, Ember. Mary Jean doesn't need anything else to distract her."

"Y'all should've seen that one coming," Rickiah said. She swiped a dollop of frosting off of her cheesecake and tasted it. She was one of the only humans in town who knew about magic. "Can't one of you see the future?"

"I don't know what you're talking about," Stevie joked. "I just see dead people."

"That would be my mother, and her dreams are sporadic," I commented.

Rickiah was well aware of all of our gifts, but she never turned down a chance to tease us about them.

"Y'all take care." Rickiah sighed and picked up her cake box. "I'll see you this weekend. Are y'all going to the kick-off party at the hotel Friday night?"

"We haven't thought that far ahead," I responded.

"All right. See you later."

I followed Rickiah out of the kitchen and opened the bakery door. As soon as she stepped into the warm evening air, I locked up for the night. The dark wood floors shined, and the scattered café tables, peach-colored walls, and wide display case at the register created the perfect ambience. The Lunar Bakery had just the right amount of southern charm all the tourists visiting the little Gulf Coast town expected. An added bonus was the gold star constellations my mom had painted on the ceiling when I was a kid.

Customers often stared at them searching for their star signs while they waited for their coffee.

"These extended hours are going to run me ragged." Stevie tucked a lock of her midnight bob behind her ear. "Let's just raise our prices."

"I think we should consider both," I said. The family bakery had been my late father's pride and joy, and I'd been responsible for the finances ever since quitting my corporate job in New York City and moving back to southern Alabama. I couldn't let the business fail.

"Both?"

"I know you're hesitant about our prices because we sell to so many locals, but I have a solution for you." I straightened my taupe-colored blouse. According to Stevie, it was a step up from my usual attire. Black. Brown. And more black.

"It'd better be good." The madder Stevie was, the more I heard her southern accent.

"We can raise our prices and offer a special discount for residents and local businesses," I suggested. "I ran all the numbers. With the added baking classes, we could easily afford to hire an assistant baker. You wouldn't have to be here every morning at five a.m. You could start taking breaks for once."

"An assistant, huh?" Stevie placed her hands on her hips.

"Orion would love it," I added.

"He's glued to his comics, but you're right. I need to get my boy out more."

"So, can I place an ad in the *Misty Messenger*?" I asked.

"I'm willing to give it a try," she agreed.

I continued cleaning the counters and making sure all of our kitchen equipment was ready for the morning. My eye caught sight of something on one of the stools. A cell phone. I picked it up, recognizing it immediately. It was Kalen's, and I had no idea when he would realize he'd left it at the bakery since he'd rushed straight to work at the Crystal Grande Hotel.

"What's that?" Stevie asked.

"Kalen left his phone."

"Such a weird guy," she muttered. "I don't want him pounding on our door late at night to get it back. If he's anything like Aqua, he probably sleeps with it."

"I'll swing by the hotel on our way home. It's a sleepy Monday night. He won't be missing out on anything."

* * *

Yogi, my dad's red bloodhound, followed me to the hotel. I clutched Kalen's phone in one hand and grinned, remembering how Yogi used to follow my dad around town while he ran errands. I'd assumed Dad's role as bakery manager and bookkeeper, and Yogi was part of the package deal.

The sun was going down and street lamps lit up Main Street, which was filled with tourist shops and colorful storefronts. Couples walked hand in hand, groups of onlookers stopped to take pictures of the indigo sky, and a long line trailed from the ice cream parlor. It was February and technically winter, but the southern heat lingered anyway.

I saw the Crystal Grande Hotel in the distance. It lit up like a beacon on the shore, and green, purple, and gold lights had already been hung for the upcoming Mardi Gras celebrations. I walked toward the beach and took deep breaths as our path got steeper. The higher we climbed, the better view I had of the beach and the calm ocean waves.

The public beach ended and the private stretch of sand belonging to the hotel began just before we reached the front entrance. As little girl, I'd often thought of the Crystal Grande as a mermaid palace with a private mermaid hideaway and seashell-shaped cupcakes. As an adult, I understood why. The historic plantation-style hotel had thick white columns and intricate balconies that rose as high as four stories. It was known for its southern charm, its award-winning restaurant that spanned the length of the first-floor patio overlooking the beach, and its famous residents, Jewel and Jonathon Carmichael.

Yogi stepped in front of me as chanting filled the night.

The entrance was blocked by a group of people holding signs.

"What on earth?" I muttered as I studied the protestors one-by-one.

"Banish the beads! Banish the beads!" Mary Jean stood at the head of the group chanting and holding a sign with a picture of Mardi Gras masks overlaid with a big red X.

A couple of valets ran in and out of the front entrance, trying to clear a pathway for guests to get through the chaos. Yogi barked at the sight. Overall, Misty Key was home to a conservative bunch. Protests like Mary Jean's didn't happen often, and hers was definitely sure to make the front page of the *Misty Messenger*.

Yogi trotted through the crowd, and I followed him into the hotel and took a deep breath. The lobby was a lot more peaceful, and, now that George Carmichael was back, it looked just as it had years ago before I'd left for New York. His portrait hung on the wall just beyond the reception desk. It looked as if it had been reframed, and a pair of lights had been installed above it to make it a more prominent feature among the wooden antique furniture.

I glanced at Mr. Carmichael's thick brows and rounded nose, and it brought back memories of the night my sisters and I had spotted him on the walking trail behind our house, thanks to Yogi's incessant barking. The next day, the Carmichaels had held a press conference announcing that the billionaire mogul George Carmichael had returned from his watery grave. The details of his return hadn't been addressed, but my sisters and I had figured he'd already been back in Misty Key for several weeks and had been sneaking in some outdoors time in the middle of the night when the town was sleeping. Yogi had barked in the night several times during those weeks.

He didn't bark in the middle of the night anymore.

Yogi nudged my calf, and I glanced at Kalen's cell phone, wondering about the best way to find him. He was most likely hanging around the employee break room somewhere. I hadn't seen him out front parking cars in the midst of the protestors.

A strange tingling moved up my spine as my eyes darted around the lobby and settled on a hallway leading to guest rooms located on the first floor. A number caught my eye, and then another. They stood out to me in the crowded foyer as if they were drenched in neon orange paint. I couldn't ignore them. The numbers made my thoughts spin, bringing up past memories and random thoughts.

It was part of my gift—interpreting people and places through numbers and sometimes letters. A common term for it was numerology. I was able to see the infinite numbers and patterns that made up the universe and shaped everyday life. I was getting better at using my gift. Some days were better than others.

But the glowing numbers in the hotel didn't need much interpretation.

They were warning me.

Fours. Lots of fours.

I gulped.

Numbers didn't lie.

I bit the inside of my cheek and jumped when the elevator dinged. A couple deep in conversation stepped off and walked toward the hotel's restaurant. My heart pounded. I placed a hand on my chest and took a deep breath. Yogi let out a soft bark as I casually scanned the lobby for anything that looked out of place. Nothing seemed off to me.

"OK, maybe I'm just seeing things." I looked down at Yogi. "Maybe I'm just tired. Sometimes I see things that aren't there when I'm tired. Even Stevie has a hard time telling whether someone is alive or dead when she's exhausted."

Yogi barked in response.

"Yes, OK." I took another deep breath. "Now I'm not making any sense. Let's just find Kalen and get out of here."

Yogi's ears perked up, and I suddenly got goose bumps up and down my forearms.

A maid came running down the very hallway where I'd seen the flashing numbers. She sprinted for the lobby with wide, teary eyes, and a look that made my heart race all over again. Her mouth was open, but she didn't make a sound until she'd reached the middle of the lobby. She dropped to the floor just a few feet from me.

The first thing out of her mouth was a bloodcurdling scream that forced everyone within earshot to stop what they were doing. Tears flooded the maid's cheeks as she buried her face in her hands. Yogi was the first one to offer comfort.

"What's the matter?" I asked, kneeling next to her. "What happened?"

The woman at the reception desk huddled over us, and a small crowd of onlookers gathered to watch. My stomach churned as I waited for the maid to wipe her eyes and calm herself down long enough to speak.

"He's...he's..." The maid breathed in short bursts.

"Take a few deep breaths," I suggested. "Close your eyes for a minute. We're here to help you, so try to calm down."

The maid nodded, trying to mend her irregular breaths. She pointed to the hallway leading to the guest rooms on the first floor.

"He's dead!" The maid forced the words from her mouth. "I went to clean the room and...he's not breathing!" She sobbed some more.

I stood up.

The numbers were still there calling out to me.

They'd marked a death at the Crystal Grande Hotel.

Chapter 2

There was no question that the man in front of me was dead.

Yogi had taken off running, and I'd followed him. We'd ended up in a corner hotel room on the first floor.

Yogi dashed from the bed to the bathroom, ignoring my pleas to sit still. The crime scene was a deluxe room with a prime view of the ocean, a sitting area, and a small dining table. The victim was lying face up on the bed and wearing a bath robe with the hotel's logo in the front. His cheeks had no color and his lips looked blue. His chest didn't move at all. I hesitated to feel his neck for a pulse. I didn't do well with the dead the way Stevie did.

I studied the man's features and quickly covered my mouth.

I recognized him.

"Oh, no," I muttered. "Yogi, we've got to get out of here. This isn't good. Yogi?"

I turned around and found Yogi up on a chair sniffing something on the dining table. A brown cake box caught my eye—a Lunar Bakery cake box—and I shook my head at the sight of a red velvet cheesecake sitting next to it. One slice had been cut and placed on a dessert plate. There was a bite missing.

My lungs felt as if they'd been turned into blocks of ice.

Footsteps filled the hallway, and I whistled at Yogi as I stepped out of the hotel room and shut the door behind me just in time to see policemen in the distance. I bowed my head quietly as they crowded the hotel room, ushering in a team of paramedics.

I walked casually back to the lobby with Yogi at my heels. I didn't make it very far before running into the one person I'd been hoping to avoid. Detective Winter spotted me right away. He wore his usual suit, sporting a blue tie that matched the ice blue color of his eyes. They seemed to glow compared to his ebony skin. Especially today.

"Ember Greene," he said, crossing his arms. His clothes were perfectly pressed and his attention to detail was convenient for police work, but inconvenient when it came to me and my sisters. "What are you doing here?"

I held up Kalen's cell phone.

"A customer left this at the bakery," I replied.

"What's the customer's name?" He pulled his cell phone from his pocket and began making a few notes.

"Do we really have to do this now?"

Detective Winter raised his eyebrows.

An officer approached him and interrupted our conversation.

"Sir, the victim is in Room 111," the officer said. "They've him pronounced dead."

"Has the victim been identified?"

"Yes." The officer hung his head. "It's Mr. George Carmichael, the owner of the hotel."

The detective nodded and gave the officer another assignment. He studied my expression and paused for a minute before continuing our conversation.

"Well, if that's all—"

"Do you care to explain what you were doing in Room 111?" The detective tilted his head and watched me carefully.

"What do you mean?"

"You saw the victim," he stated. "My officer confirmed that George Carmichael was dead, and you didn't even flinch."

I exhaled loudly.

"That maid ran into the lobby screaming," I admitted. "And Yogi here took off running." I patted the top of his head and he sat patiently by my side. "Don't worry. I didn't touch anything."

"I see." He glanced at his phone and typed a few things. "That's all I need for now."

I cleared my throat and eyed the exit. "Best of luck to you, Detective."

My first encounter with Detective Winter hadn't gone so well. Neither had the second. Or the third. The townsfolk often commented that he had a heart made of ice, and I'd also believed that to be true until last month when he'd surprised me by helping out with a problem at the town's annual craft fair.

"And you," he added. "You'll be seeing me soon. Don't leave town."

OK, maybe there's still a bit of ice in there somewhere.

* * *

The next morning, I awoke to an angry phone call from Stevie. I arrived at the bakery before opening just as Detective Winter's men were searching the kitchen from top to bottom. Detective Winter observed the scene wearing his usual unwrinkled slacks and button-down. There was no hint of weariness in his eyes, and he hadn't stared once at the espresso machine.

Sometimes I wondered if he was a machine that ate, slept, and breathed police work.

"I have customers to serve, you know," Stevie shouted at one of the officers as he poked at the pastries she'd already made for the morning rush. Her attention shifted to another officer looking through an assortment of pans next to the ovens. "For the love of sweet tea, be careful with those!"

"Is this really necessary?" I scowled at the detective.

"One of *your* cakes was found at the crime scene, and we have reason to believe it was used to kill the victim," he replied.

"It wasn't a cake," I muttered. "It was a red velvet cheesecake."

"And *we* didn't make it," Stevie added, placing her hands on her hips. "That was a special project for the students in my baking course. I haven't sold a red velvet cheesecake since last year."

"Then how did that cheesecake end up in Room 111?" The detective looked at me and then at Stevie.

"I don't know, Detective," Stevie answered. "But I supervised every one of my students, and there was nothing fishy going on in my kitchen. If that cheesecake was poisoned, it was poisoned after it left the bakery."

"I understand that." The detective watched an officer return from the storage pantry and shake his head. "But we have to explore every possibility. That red velvet cheesecake is being tested as we speak. If that dessert tests positive for a deadly substance, it doesn't look good for either of you."

"Detective Winter, you can't be serious." Stevie glared at him, something she did often. The focused staring came across as intimidating to most, but it was her way of focusing on the living, rather than the rambling of the dead going on in the background.

"I need a list of your students, please." He pulled out his cell phone and glanced at Stevie.

Stevie clenched her jaw and muttered a few swear words as she watched another officer rearrange the contents of her fridge.

"It's our first round of students," I answered on Stevie's behalf. "There are six of them."

"Names?" He raised his eyebrows.

"There's Rickiah Pepper, a good friend of mine," I answered. "She had nothing to do with this. I'm one hundred percent certain."

"I don't need your opinion, Ms. Greene." The detective paused and cleared his throat. "All I need are names."

"R-i-c-k-i-a-h," I continued. "She hates it when her name is spelled wrong. There's Darlene Johnston. She owns the antiques shop down the street. Kalen Haywood works as a valet at the hotel. Cindy Buford owns that playhouse just off of Main Street. Zinny Pellman works for the *Misty Messenger*, and then there's Mary Jean Covey."

"Thank you." Detective Winter finished documenting each name.

"What are you going to do?" I watched the detective wave at one of his officers.

"Invite myself in for a slice of cheesecake." For the first time, the detective cracked a half-smile. It left me speechless. I stared at him, wondering what he was really like when he was off-duty. "It was a joke, Ms. Greene."

"Oh." I nodded. "Right. Of course."

"You'll be hearing from me," he added. His serious expression returned, and he tilted his head toward the exit.

I stood wide-eyed as Detective Winter and the rest of his men wrapped up their search and promptly left the bakery. As soon as they did, Stevie paced around the kitchen with her hands on her hips. She let out a low growl as she glanced at the sink.

"Great," she muttered. "Now I have to sanitize just about everything we own. Did you see that officer stick his grubby little hands in our pastry case?" She wrinkled her nose. "So far, these baking classes are doing more harm than good."

"They won't shut down the bakery." I took a deep breath and weighed the odds in my head. My heart raced. If that red velvet cheesecake tested positive for something lethal, we were all in trouble. I tried to hide my concerns by keeping a straight face.

"Are you sure?"

"Well..."

"Exactly," Stevie responded. "All Detective Winter has to do is snap his fingers and our family legacy is gone." She rolled her eyes and glanced at the time. We had a lot of work to do before our morning customers arrived.

"It won't come to that." My stomach churned just thinking about it. I hoped I was right.

"Don't be stupid, Ember. We're on thin ice this time. The thinnest we've ever been on."

I glimpsed out the window. "We've been in jams before. We'll survive."

Someone had to stay positive, and that someone apparently wasn't going to be Stevie.

"Sure." Stevie leaned against a counter and stared at the shiny kitchen floor. "But that doesn't change the fact that there's a killer waltzing around right under our noses."

The thought hit me like a ten-pound bag of flour to the face.

"Then we'll figure out what happened," I commented. "All we have to do is track down all of those red velvet cheesecakes."

"That still doesn't change the fact that one of my students is a murderer." She kept her head down, glaring at the tennis shoes she wore to work every day. They'd seen better days. "Cake classes. What was I thinking? I can't believe I let you talk me into this."

I gulped, my heart still pounding.

I'd failed my family once—no way could I fail them again.

If the bakery shut down or even lost business because of the murder case, I didn't know how I would handle it. Stevie was right. The baking course had been my idea, and now we were in a tight spot because of it.

I took a deep breath. "These classes still have the potential to pull the business up to new heights. This is just a temporary setback."

Stevie finally looked up and rubbed underneath her eyes. "What the cosmos are you smoking, sis? Is money all you care about? There won't be a business to build if that cheesecake tests positive."

"If anyone can figure out what really happened to George Carmichael, it's us. We interact with each suspect on a regular basis."

"It sounds risky. I don't want to dig us a deeper grave." She crossed her arms and gave me one of her domineering glares.

"We have no choice," I pointed out.

"Fine." She clenched her jaw and continued glaring. "But if we lose the bakery, I'm holding *you* personally responsible."

Chapter 3

Stevie was a firm believer that bad news came in threes.

A death.

A poisoned red velvet cheesecake from our bakery.

And then there was Nova, our regional representative.

She'd decided to visit during one of our usual afternoon lulls, and she held a soft, black carrier in one hand along with her oversized handbag—a shade of pink that matched her lipstick. Nova handed me the carrier as soon as she saw me. It didn't weigh much, and I carefully inspected every inch. When I came to a mesh window on one side, I peeked into the carrier. Two yellow eyes stared back at me. My heart jumped.

Nova had brought a cat to the bakery.

"Uh, what is this?" I stared at Nova, confused. Stevie studied the black carrier and crossed her arms, refusing to take it off my hands.

"We'd better sit down," Nova replied.

The three of us sat at a quiet café table in the corner. I placed the carrier on the floor, hoping it was just one of Nova's new companions. Aqua and our only other employee, Luann Watts, manned the register as I sat next to Stevie. As Nova situated herself, Aqua brought us all coffees and chocolate croissants.

Nova carefully clasped her hands together. Her auburn hair was up in a tight bun, and her glimmering silver earrings were shaped like cats. She glanced down at her morning pastry and automatically added extra cream to her coffee. She rarely ate in front of us. Because her psychic talent was tied to food, she tended to make people feel uncomfortable around meal and snack times.

"What's going on?" I asked. "What's with the cat?"

"You did receive a letter from the Clairs, did you not?" She raised her eyebrows.

Stevie averted her gaze to an empty space at the edge of the table and rolled her eyes.

"Yes, we received the letter about our next case," I answered.

Stevie kept her eyes on the edge of the table. I couldn't see anything, but I knew what she was looking at. It was the very reason Yogi had decided to wait for me in my office instead of snoozing at my feet during out meeting. Stevie claimed that a Siamese cat followed Nova wherever she went.

According to Stevie, the cat was pesky and patronizing.

Also, it was dead.

"Good." Nova leaned back slightly. "Then you know it is of the utmost importance that you two go to Cottonberry as soon as possible." She pursed her lips and pulled a folder full of papers from her giant purse. "A new family of witches, the Hextons, just moved in next to the Grants. They claim the Grants kidnapped their familiar."

"I'm guessing this familiar is a cat?" I glanced down at the black carrier.

"A black cat," Nova clarified. "He goes by the name of Whiskers."

"No," Stevie stated. "Absolutely not."

"I haven't even finished explaining." Nova narrowed her eyes.

"We're Seers. I'm not babysitting that thing because a bunch of spellcasters got into an argument." Stevie shook her head.

"You are up to date on section eighteen of the handbook, right?" Nova straightened her shoulders and eyed the folder full of papers.

"Yes." I grabbed a coffee and took a small sip.

"Good," she continued. "Then you know that neither party can possess an item of conflict until an agreement is signed, or in this case, Whiskers doesn't have a home until you fix this."

"And if the Grants and the Hextons can't come to an agreement?" The carrier on the floor wiggled, and my heart jumped again.

"Whiskers will have to find another witching family to serve," she responded. "So, I suggest y'all head to Cottonberry as soon as possible."

"Don't the Grants have the brains to resolve this on their own?" Stevie's eyes darted over her shoulder where Aqua was making an iced coffee. She hadn't touched her hot cup of joe. Sweet tea was more her thing. "I mean, it's just a cat."

"You know very well it's not just a cat." Nova touched a piece of her croissant. "A witch's familiar serves a very important purpose."

"I know." Stevie's eyes fixated on a new spot at the table. I assumed she was looking at the dead Siamese cat again. "They're little mischief makers."

"They're loyal family companions," Nova corrected her. "And it's not very often that they just show up at your front door."

"Is that what Whiskers did?" I asked.

Nova nodded. "He presented himself to the Hexton family, but the Grants claim Whiskers already belonged to them. They don't have much evidence to support this, unfortunately."

"Any magical powers?" I raised my eyebrows and wondered what we were in for as I watched the carrier wiggle some more.

"None have been reported."

"Then let the cat decide." Stevie shrugged, finally pulling her gaze away from the dead Siamese. "There you go. Problem solved."

"Do what you must." Nova tore a piece of croissant and sniffed it. "All you have to do is document everything."

"Looks like you have things covered." Stevie glanced at the register again and slowly rose from her chair.

Our last visit to Cottonberry, Alabama, hadn't gone well.

In fact, Stevie had almost lost her leg.

"Sit, please," Nova instructed. "You're one of our best Seers, Stevie. You've never been this reluctant to take on a new case. What's the problem here?"

I glanced at my sister. I knew the answer to that question, but it wasn't my tale to tell. Stevie cleared her throat and stayed standing. She bit the side of her lip, her expression turning cold.

She loathed witches and warlocks.

Well...*one* warlock in particular.

I didn't know any more details than that.

"No problem," Stevie lied. "I'm just extremely busy."

"You're always extremely busy," she pointed out. Stevie shrugged again and remained silent. "Then you give me no choice. I know you made these croissants."

Nova studied the piece of golden croissant in her hand and took a bite.

Her eating habits sometimes made others uncomfortable because her gift was clairgustance. It was one of the six clairs, and it was a talent I'd heard about but had never seen for myself until last year. It was the ability to read and interpret someone's energy by taste. Nova had explained to me once that she used to taste things sporadically without ever putting anything in her mouth. Eventually her gift had developed into something more. She could read people and places by tasting a food within close proximity. She'd once told me there was an infinite amount of psychic energy surrounding food—everything from the emotional state of the cook to the thoughts of those eating the dish. It was a talent I didn't fully understand, but it was comical to watch.

"No, don't give me a reading, Nova. I'm really not in the mood to have someone dig deep into my personal life." Stevie scratched the side of her head. Her nostrils flared as she observed Nova chewing slowly. Nova stared straight ahead as if she were watching a movie of Stevie's life play out in front of her.

"OK, I get it." Nova placed the croissant back on her plate. "You have a lot of conflicting feelings surrounding the Grant family. You hate seeing them because they bring back painful memories. Is this correct?"

"So much for privacy." Stevie snatched the rest of Nova's croissant.

"I could say more," she added. "You practically baked all of your troubles into that pastry."

"Fine." Stevie glanced around the bakery and lowered her voice. "OK. I admit it. I don't like the Grants, and I don't like Cottonberry."

"Making peace with the past so you can move forward is part of being a Seer." Nova nodded matter-of-factly. "That's basically what we do for the magical community. We heal. We mediate. We provide closure. We do all of these things to help people get on with their lives and live in peace."

"The Seer Handbook, page seven," I added. "A direct quote. That's pretty impressive."

"I'm aware of what the handbook says." Stevie took a deep breath. "And I disagree. There are some things you can *never* get over. Some things in life you just have to deal with until the day you die. I'm not going to Cottonberry again, and that's final. Ember can go with Aqua. In fact, let Aqua talk to the cat and then take him back to his family of choice."

"Aqua just started her training," Nova replied. "And, technically, two licensed Seers are needed for a mediation. The paperwork would be a nightmare otherwise."

"Oh, I would hate to burden you with more paperwork," Stevie sarcastically answered. She clutched the pastry plate tighter and walked back into the kitchen.

A minute of silence passed over the table while I tried to guess Nova's thoughts. She'd given me a reading once, and she'd been spot on. Stevie's reading also didn't disappoint. I looked over my shoulder at the variety of pastries, muffins, bars, and cookies behind the glass near the register.

"You can certainty tell a lot from a little croissant," I said.

"Since Stevie made them, it was a cake walk." She chuckled briefly at her own choice of words.

"What about people who suck at baking?" I pointed to myself. "My mama's microwave is currently my best friend."

"That's simple," she explained. "I just have them serve me something like you did last year. I can still get a reading that way, although it's a little more cryptic."

"You know why she hates the Grants, don't you?"

"Yes." She tilted her head. "I just didn't want to bombard her with too many details."

I scanned the table, wondering what her ghost cat was up to now.

"It's my nephew, Orion." Orion was the spitting image of his mother in most ways. Although none of us knew where he'd gotten his bright blue eyes. "He's ten years old, and Stevie won't tell anyone who his father is. I've always had a sneaking suspicion that he's a warlock. You didn't happen to see anything about it, did you?"

"I did see something," she said quietly. She opened her mouth but then closed it again, hesitating to give me an answer.

"Whatever it is, you have to tell me, Nova," I whispered. "She's my sister."

"Can you convince her to go to Cottonberry with you? You know the protocol." She eyed the front door as the bell chimed and a few more customers entered for their afternoon java fix. "It was such a headache last year getting you approved to work Aqua's kidnapping case with an expired Seer license. I can't call in any more favors. I'm all out."

"I understand," I replied. "I'll talk to her, but I can't promise anything."

"Thank you." She took a deep breath, handed me the folder full of paper, grabbed her oversized handbag, and stood to leave. "Take care of Whiskers. He really is no trouble."

"Wait." I jumped to my feet. "You owe me a tidbit of info, remember?"

"I shouldn't meddle." Nova lifted her chin and took a step toward the exit.

I grabbed her arm.

"I do something for you, and you do something for me," I muttered. "That's how this works. Besides, how can any of us help her heal if we have no idea what kind of wounds we're dealing with?"

Nova yanked her arm away.

"All right." She pursed her lips, studying Luann at the front counter as she took a customer's order. "I didn't see who the father was, but I did see something else."

"What?"

"The Grants know who he is."

"Maybe because the father is their son Warner?"

"Maybe." Nova shrugged. "Maybe not. Stevie keeps those details locked away. That's all I know."

As Nova walked confidently out the door and into the Alabama sun, I turned to the carrier on the floor. It wiggled a little more, and I quickly grabbed the handle. I headed back to my office, wondering how Yogi would react. I stopped when I saw Aqua in the kitchen refilling a plate of cookies.

My little sister had just received her crest reading from Lady Deja, and she'd decided to pursue her Seer license. Lady Deja, the head of the Clairs, had announced Aqua's psychic talent not too long ago. She was a pet psychic in training, which explained how she knew so much about the random behaviors of the family dog.

"Aqua," I muttered. "Come here."

"Yeah." Aqua tossed her long braid over her shoulder. Her hair was the same shade of caramel as mine, but she liked to experiment with hair dye. Her latest venture was purple streaks.

I slowly unzipped the black carrier. Whiskers immediately popped his head out and studied his new surroundings. His big yellow eyes fixated on me first and then on Aqua.

"It's time for you to practice your gift."

Chapter 4

"His name is Whiskers." I pulled Aqua into my office and shut the door. Yogi immediately stood up and began sniffing. I clenched my fists, hoping he wouldn't growl.

"Hello, little Whiskers." Aqua's voice went up an octave as if she was speaking to a toddler.

Whiskers slowly exited the carrier and looked around the room. His wide yellow eyes settled on Yogi first. He didn't even flinch. Yogi took a few steps closer and then retreated back to his regular napping spot underneath my desk. I breathed a sigh of relief.

If Yogi didn't mind him, Whiskers couldn't be all that bad.

"OK, do your thing," I said.

"I'm trying." Aqua knelt down and began petting the cat. He rubbed against her calves and waved his tail in the air.

"Ask him what happened," I continued. "Ask him if he belongs to the Grants or the Hextons."

"What do you think, little guy?" Aqua frowned as she studied Whiskers. "Where did you come from? Who do you belong to?"

Aqua sat in silence for a few minutes. Her gaze followed Whiskers as he carefully explored the rest of the office. Aqua scratched her head, which wasn't very reassuring. I sighed and sat down at my desk.

I shrugged? "Anything?" I wanted to get the Cottonberry case off of my plate as soon as possible so I could focus on saving the family business before Stevie had a breakdown.

"I don't understand," she answered. "I'm not getting anything from him. Nothing at all."

"How often do you know what Yogi is thinking?"

She watched him doze off. "All the time."

"Then you should be able to communicate with Whiskers too, right?"

"I don't know." She tugged at her purple braid and stood up. "Yogi has been around since I was little. Maybe that's why I understand him so well. Or maybe my talent won't do much until I'm old like you."

"*Old?*" I wrinkled my nose, suddenly a little too conscious of the creases it made on my forehead. I gently touched the front of my head. "I'm not old."

"Stevie said it's all downhill once you hit thirty," she commented.

"Stevie would say that." I straightened my shoulders, also aware of my poor posture. "But I'll have you know your thirties are way better than your twenties because—"

"You have life all figured out?" Aqua grinned as she looked me up and down.

"Yeah." I sighed. The truth sucked to admit. My love life was a bust, and I was currently living with my mother. Up until last year, I'd had a career in the city and held a position of some importance.

I'd tossed that one aside too.

"I have to help Luann with customers, and I have night school tonight," Aqua said.

"We'll try again later." I snuck a glimpse at Whiskers. He'd jumped up on top of the filing cabinet. "Maybe you'll pick up on something once he's been here for a while. He could just be the quiet type."

"I hope you're right." Aqua raised her eyebrows, looking at Whiskers one last time.

Aqua left the office, and I went back to combing through special orders and emails. I clicked on an email confirming my ad for a baking assistant. I skimmed the ad a few times before approving it to be published in the next issue of the *Misty Messenger*.

My cell phone buzzed, and Yogi perked up for a second. I looked at my phone, shocked to see a number I hadn't seen in months. My heart pounded as I cleared my throat and answered it with as much poise as I could.

"Hello?"

"Ember?" My old boss Mr. Cohen sounded even more haggard than usual. That was common for a man in his position. His hair had been a solid shade of brown when I'd first started at Fillmore Media. By the time I'd sent in my notice last year, his hair had morphed into a solid shade of gray.

"Mr. Cohen," I responded. "What a surprise."

"We're very busy over here, Ember, so I'm going to cut to the chase." He coughed to clear his throat. "I want you back on the team."

I thought for a moment before responding. A part of me wanted to accept his offer right away, but I couldn't leave my family again.

Especially not now.

"That's very flattering, but I'm not interested in my old position," I answered. I nodded reassuringly at my reflection in the computer screen.

"I know," he went on. "That's why I'm calling to offer you the position Mr. Fillmore should have given you in the first place. You have a way with numbers, and I want you to be our new Director of Finance."

I held the phone away from my ear and tried to collect my thoughts. My chest pounded as a million memories raced through my head. I'd worked hard for that position only to lose it to one of my coworkers. I took a deep breath, not knowing how to respond.

"I thought that position was taken," I finally said.

"The last guy couldn't handle it." He paused for a second. "Take a few days to think about it."

"Look, Mr. Cohen—"

"Unless you've found another employer who appreciates your work?" He waited again, but I didn't know how to reply. Almost everything I'd done to try to help the bakery had been a fight with Stevie every step of the way. Change was a difficult pill to swallow, but waiting for the dust to settle every week had been exhausting.

"Um—"

"That's what I thought," he cut in. "I can't imagine you're happy living in whatever mud hole it is you're from."

"Misty Key is nice place."

"Don't get me wrong," he continued. "I'm sure it's good for visiting, but New York City is a one-of-a-kind town. Unless you just couldn't cut it around here, a small-town girl like yourself?"

"I handled it just fine." I frowned. "You sure have a funny way of delivering job offers."

"Oh, you know what I'm getting at. I can only give you a week to think about it. The salary is almost twice what you were making, and you'll get the corner office on the top floor."

"OK, I'll think about it," I said.

"Please do." Mr. Cohen hung up, and I stared at my phone.

Yogi stared at me.

"I swear someone is messing with me," I stated.

Yogi let out a soft bark.

"I busted my butt for that director job, and now that I've moved on with my life, my old boss basically wants to hand it to me on a silver platter. Can you believe that?"

He whined in response.

"I know. I thought I was over New York too." I placed a hand on my chest. My heart was still racing, and I couldn't stop imagining myself in that coveted office surrounded by envious eyes.

I guess I *wasn't* over my old life in the city.

Chapter 5

Stevie had exceeded her usual amount of snappiness when she snatched my box of assorted cookies. I rolled my eyes and held up my hands in surrender. I'd grabbed a few of our leftovers from the bakery and packed them nicely in a box for Mrs. Johnston.

"You have a habit of dropping things," Stevie muttered.

"Is this really about a box of cookies?"

Stevie huffed as she walked ahead of me toward the antiques shop.

It was a humid evening, and Main Street was lit up like a fairground. Groups of locals, tourists, and hand-holding couples filled the sidewalks. There was a line out the door at the ice cream parlor, as always, and laughter and live music came from several of the bars.

Stevie stopped when she reached Darlene Johnston's shop. The windows were dark except for a lingering light on in the back. A mannequin in the window displayed a short, plum-colored dress and matching hat from the 1920s. It stood alongside an antique wooden chair and a stack of old-fashioned trunks.

I knocked on the door and waved at Darlene as soon as she came into view.

Stevie and I exchanged nervous glances as Darlene unlocked the door looking surprised to see us.

I forced a smile and pushed aside my lingering thoughts of New York City and the director position. I nudged Stevie, and she handed Darlene the box of cookies.

"I know how you love those Bama cookies," I commented. "Can we come in?"

"Of course." She glanced over her shoulder and opened the door further. Stevie and I walked inside. "Just give me a minute to clear away the clutter in my office."

Darlene hurried to the back of the store, and I followed right behind her.

"You don't have to clean on our account," I said.

Stevie cleared her throat and glanced at a darkened corner decorated with bookcases. She raised her eyebrows and all at once, my stomach churned.

"Distract her," Stevie whispered. "I just spotted someone."

"A—"

"Yes, a ghost," she murmured. Stevie walked deeper into the shadowy shop, and my skin crawled just thinking about being in the same room as a spirit. Stevie didn't seem to mind.

I walked into Darlene's office just as she scooped up a pile of papers and shoved them into her desk drawer.

"Wow." I looked around the room. Antiques and knickknacks filled every corner. "So this is where the magic happens."

"Sometimes I go weeks without new inventory, and sometimes I get tons of new items all at once."

Darlene moved to an old dresser that took up the space next to her computer. The wood was dark, and the brass knobs looked as if they needed a good cleaning. My eyes darted to a shelf on the opposite end of the office. My toes curled when I saw dozens of eyes looking back at me.

"Oh my," I whispered.

"Porcelain dolls," Darlene commented. "Collectors love them. Where's Stevie?"

"I think she got stuck looking at that vintage kitchen equipment you have by the register," I lied.

"That olive-colored fridge does get lots of attention, although no buyer as of yet."

"I bet." I maneuvered around stacks of books and magazines to get to the nearest chair.

"What can I do for you?" Darlene asked. "Did I leave something at the bakery yesterday?"

"No." I waved a hand. "No. I just..." I looked at the door, wondering how long Stevie planned on chasing the dead. "I just wanted to see how you're liking the baking course. And we had the extra cookies."

"My grandkids will gobble them up." She smiled and tucked a strand of her honey brown hair behind her ear. Bangs sat just above her eyebrows, and she always curled them in like she did to the ends of her hair.

"I'm sure they'll enjoy that red velvet cheesecake too," Stevie said as she joined the conversation. She gently rested her hand on the nearest piece of furniture. I couldn't decipher whether or not her discussion with the dead had been a successful one. She had yet to make eye contact with me.

"Yes, Harold had a slice last night," Darlene commented. "It was love at first bite. I told him to make it last another week, but I don't think it will."

"So, that cheesecake is in your fridge at home?" I asked.

Darlene tilted her head and chuckled. "Yes. Why do you ask?"

I cleared my throat. "Stevie, I was just telling Darlene we wanted her thoughts on the baking course."

"Right." Stevie nodded, her eyes darting around the room and stopping when she too spotted the shelf of porcelain dolls. "How are you liking it? I mean, so far?"

"I'm liking it just fine." She looked from Stevie to me. "Is that really what you're here to ask me about?"

My chest went tight.

I wasn't about to admit to Darlene that we suspected her of murder.

But if her cheesecake was where she'd said it was, she was as innocent as Yogi.

"No." Stevie hung her head. My eyes went wide. "It's the...um...you have cats, right?"

"Three." Her confused expression brightened immediately. "Cherry, Tansy, and Bobo."

"Good, because we found a stray, and we could use some pointers," Stevie said. "And food. We need to borrow some cat food."

"You should have just said so." Darlene waded through the clutter near her desk. "You'll need a litter box, and make sure you leave out fresh water every day. Oh, and don't let him or her get into anything with onion or garlic."

"Good to know." I nodded.

"I'll meet you two out front." Darlene headed for the exit. "I have some food you can take home with you. I leave a bag here for when Bobo comes to work with me. He has some separation anxiety."

Stevie and I followed Darlene back into the darkened shop. Darlene went to retrieve her extra cat food, and I inched slowly toward the front door. Stevie's eyes darted from corner to corner, but nothing seemed to pique her interest.

"She claims her cheesecake is at home," I whispered.

"She could be lying."

"Darlene? Lie?" I looked over my shoulder. "She didn't seem like she was lying to me. What about you? Any ghostly luck?"

"No." She sighed. "Just a bunch of loonies attached to their trinkets." She turned her head as if one was currently speaking to her. "They're all over this place. It's surprising the amount of people who can't let stuff go."

"Here you go." Darlene appeared from the back of the shop holding a plastic bag. She handed it to me.

"This should be enough for a few days. Let me know if you can't find the owner. I have more than enough room at home, and Harold doesn't mind."

"Thank you." I smiled and waited for Darlene to let us out.

Stevie and I stood quietly on Main Street as Darlene went back inside her shop. The sidewalks were a little less busy, and the sky was a deep indigo blue. Stars twinkled overhead, and the sound of faint music and laughter danced through the humid night air.

Stevie started our trek back home but stopped suddenly in front of Darlene's display window. Her eyes went wide as she stared straight ahead. She opened her mouth, muttering a few words. The sight sent shivers up my spine, and an unusually cool breeze circled us.

Then the breeze was gone.

Stevie took a few steps backward.

"OK," she breathed. "That was interesting."

"What?"

"I just saw a spirit," she explained. "She's gone now, but I think it was Darlene's great-grandmother or something. That was strange. Family members usually appear when I'm talking to a relative. You know, it's their way of trying to get messages to loved ones."

"What did she say?"

Judging by the glassed-over look she'd had on her face, I guessed it wasn't a pleasant encounter.

"It wasn't good." Stevie bit the side of her lip and looked up and down the street.

"Anything about the murder case?"

"She just warned me to leave Darlene alone," Stevie said.

"Why would she say that?" I narrowed my eyes, trying to put my finger on a specific reason. The only one I could come up with was that the ghost of Darlene's great-grandmother didn't approve of psychics or the magical community. She must have been ultra-conservative.

"Because, according to her dead relative, Darlene is a sinner."

Chapter 6

"I want that cat out of here, and I want him out now."

Stevie leaned against the kitchen counter with a glass of sweet tea in her hand. We'd come home from the antiques shop to a quiet house. My mom was sitting at the kitchen table with one of her magazines, and Orion was finishing up his bedtime snack. Aqua entered the room wearing pajama pants and a tank top. She was texting furiously.

Whiskers sat quietly in the corner, observing the five of us while Yogi lay sprawled out on the tile.

"Yogi likes him," I pointed out.

"Yogi also licks the trash can." Stevie took a sip of her tea and glared at Whiskers.

Orion giggled. "He's smart. Garbage is everywhere, so he'll never starve."

"Don't even think about it, hon." Stevie focused on her son. "I don't want to see or hear about any more of your weird little experiments. Humans don't eat garbage, OK?"

"Yeah they do. They eat all kinds of gross stuff like bugs and chalk and moldy cheese and—"

"Off to bed." Stevie pointed toward the staircase. "You have school in the morning, and remember what Mrs. Roche said."

"No catching bugs at recess and hiding them in my desk," he recited. "Yeah. Yeah. I know."

"And?" Stevie raised her eyebrows.

"And my teacher's name is Mrs. Roche, not Mrs. *Roach*," he added.

"Thank you."

My mom rubbed Orion's back as he stood up and trudged upstairs to his room.

"You shouldn't be so hard on him, dear," my mom said. She tugged gently on the moonstone she always wore around her neck. The dainty silver chain with its pearly stone was a family heirloom she'd always joked she would leave to her favorite daughter when she died.

"I just want him to be normal, Ma. What's so wrong about that?"

"Uh, he *isn't* normal," Aqua chimed in, still staring at her phone. "He's a Greene."

"I have no idea if he even has a psychic gift." Stevie shook her head at Aqua. "And put that thing down if you plan on being in this conversation. It's like you're in two places at once."

"It's called multi-tasking, Stevie."

"There's no such thing," she argued.

"Then explain how I got an A in physics class." She continued texting as she spoke. "I practically binge-watched an entire season of *Bonbon Voyage* during those lectures."

"The reality cooking show?" I commented. "I'm not a fan of that chef guy who hosts it."

"Enough, you two," Mom blurted out. "I've had my fill of negative vibes today. That murder at the Crystal Grande is all anyone can talk about." She took a deep breath and retreated to the kitchen cabinet above the sink where she kept spare candles. Lighting candles and meditating was her nightly ritual. The subtle scent of vanilla and lavender often wafted through the house during stressful times.

"What about the red velvet cheesecake?" I asked.

"The police have managed to keep that a secret for now," she answered.

"At least they've got one thing right," Stevie muttered.

"Well, Darlene is off the hook," I commented. "Her cheesecake is tucked away safely in her fridge."

"Unless she's lying." Stevie casually refilled her sweet tea and hovered over Aqua's shoulder. Aqua quickly maneuvered so that Stevie couldn't read her texts.

My mind jumped back to Stevie's run-in with Darlene's dead relative in front of her antiques shop. Darlene might have been hiding something, but I couldn't believe it was murder.

"We'll visit Zinny next," I said. "She'll probably have more details than us regarding the Carmichael case. I bet she's snooping around the Crystal Grande as we speak. Nothing beats a Carmichael on the front page of the local newspaper."

"You mean a *dead* Carmichael," Aqua added. "Don't be surprised if reporters and photographers start showing up from all over the country trying to get an exclusive."

"Uh, can we please acknowledge the black cat in the room here?" Stevie was back to glaring at Whiskers.

Yogi followed my mom to the sink as she cleared away Orion's glass and crumb-filled plate.

"Yeah about that." Aqua sighed and placed her phone on the table. It buzzed a few times with replies from her friends. "You have to go, Stevie, because I can't. Class was brutal tonight, and I have a big test coming up this weekend. I really need to get it out of the way so I can go to that Mardi Gras kick-off party at the hotel on Friday night."

"How convenient." Stevie set her glass of sweet tea on the counter and crossed her arms. Her bubbling hatred for Cottonberry and all it entailed made the otherwise white and bright kitchen seem glum.

"Go tomorrow afternoon," Mom suggested. "I'm sure Whiskers doesn't like you any more than you like him, Stevie. Cats are perceptive that way."

"Ma, I have a bakery to run."

"I'll cover you," she said.

"But—"

"Stevie, your father and I built that place, and I'll have Aqua and Luann to help me," she insisted. "We'll survive without you."

Stevie looked at me, and I shrugged.

"What do you say?" I tilted my head toward Whiskers, who hadn't caused any problems so far. In fact, there had been times I'd completely forgotten he was in the room. "He hasn't touched his food. We need to get him back where he belongs."

"You'll do the talking?" Stevie rubbed the ink on her forearm. It was one of her nervous habits. That and shouting.

"All I need is your signature saying that you witnessed it all."

"Simple as that, huh?" Stevie stared down at the kitchen floor for a moment. "Too bad Aqua can't communicate with him. We could ship him off tonight."

"I've tried like a million times." Aqua rolled her eyes. "I don't know what else to do. Either he's incredibly stubborn or I suck at being a pet psychic."

Aqua studied Whiskers and rubbed her forehead.

"Well—"

"Not now, Stevie," my mom interjected. Stevie and Aqua could bicker back and forth for days if no one stepped in to stop them. "Aqua, we've all been through this. You'll get better at using your gift with time. When I was your age, I was lucky if I had a prophetic dream once a month."

"Yeah." She twirled a strand of caramel hair and dove right back into answering text messages.

"Tomorrow afternoon then," I confirmed. "We'll spend the night in a hotel and drive home early Thursday morning."

The drive was a few hours, and I had a lot to think about.

"OK, but don't blame me if they refuse to work with us."

"Why would they refuse to work with you?" My mom wrinkled her nose and reached down to scratch behind Yogi's ears.

"Last time we went there, I said a few things," Stevie confessed. "Some not-so-nice things about their son and his...*broomstick*."

I laughed, remembering the horrified look on Mrs. Grant's face.

"It's been a while," I responded. "I doubt they'll remember."

Chapter 7

Stevie stuck her tongue out as we passed the sign welcoming us to Cottonberry.

Driving through central Alabama reminded me of my college days. I drove past a bustling campus and a large administrative building with red brick and a clock tower that overlooked its students. A street full of old-fashioned storefronts sat right next to campus, and not far from that was the chapel and graveyard where Stevie and I had gotten into trouble during our last visit. Looking in that direction made me cringe.

I glanced in the rearview mirror at the soft black carrier where Whiskers had sat quietly the entire drive. He still hadn't eaten anything. Aqua had tried one last time to communicate with him before we'd left the bakery. She hadn't had any luck.

"They know we're coming, right?" Stevie slouched in her seat. I'd insisted on driving since I didn't know what sort of mood she would be in once we passed the first Cottonberry road sign. She was an emotional driver.

"All I know is what's in the folder Nova gave us," I answered. "A meeting has been scheduled for this evening at the Grants'. All they know is that two Seers will be arriving to mediate."

"Prepare for quite the show."

"At least you took my advice and wore something sensible," I commented, glancing at her jeans and nude blouse. It wasn't her usual uniform of a tank top and shorts.

"Long sleeves? I'm sure I look insane. Who wears long sleeves when it's this hot?"

"Hiding your tats will give Mrs. Grant one less thing to complain about," I explained. I'd followed my own advice and picked a sensible outfit too. Although it wasn't that difficult since most of my wardrobe was black, white, tan, and meant for colder weather.

"More like one less thing to *witch* about," she muttered.

I took a deep breath. It was February, and I'd turned on the air conditioner. The sky was bathed in shades of dark pink and pretty soon the town of Cottonberry would be housed underneath a starry backdrop. I only hoped we'd be snug in our hotel room by then. I'd booked us an inexpensive room near the freeway entrance.

"OK, I'm only going to say this once." My heart started to race. As we neared the Grants' neighborhood, I questioned whether or not my timing was right. But it never felt like the right time to ask Stevie about one thing in particular.

The father of her son.

"Why do I have the feeling you're about to pry?"

"I'm not defending the Grants, and I'm not saying I support the sometimes shady business dealings of Wisteria, Inc., but what do you have against witches? I know you dated Warner Grant in high school—"

"Briefly," she quickly added.

"Yes," I continued. "But you're leaving something out. A couple of bad dates isn't enough to loathe the city of Cottonberry the way you do."

Stevie clenched her jaw, and I braced myself for the same reactions I'd gotten from her in the past. The yelling. The *mind your own business* routine. The vague stories about how all witches and warlocks were selfish human beings.

I wasn't sure why I'd even bothered asking anymore.

"Is this about what Nova said?" Stevie's voice stayed calm like she'd been expecting me to bring it up.

"Maybe?"

"I know what she said to you," Stevie admitted.

I gripped the steering wheel tighter.

"How do you know that?"

"Benny told me," she replied.

"Who?"

"This dead guy who used to work at the marina," she casually explained. "He spends a lot of time at the bakery. Don't ask me why. He told me that Nova saw more during my reading."

"So, are you going to explain?" I stared straight ahead and hoped she'd finally be brave enough to talk about it. "You know I can keep a secret."

"That's not what's stopping me, Ember." She turned and glanced out the window. "It's something else."

I turned a corner, and she instantly became more rigid. The Grant family lived in a grandiose neighborhood filled with historic homes and pristinely manicured lawns. I slowed down as we approached one of the largest ones on the block. It was a white Georgian home with gray shutters and a few cars parked in the driveway—newer and nicer cars than ours.

"Those must be the Hextons," I said as I stopped the car, getting a glimpse of several people sitting in one of the vehicles.

A man and woman stepped out of the car, and another woman who looked to be in her thirties got out of the backseat. The Hextons had bronze skin almost as dark as my friend Rickiah's, and the three of them looked as if they'd come from a long day at the beach.

Compared to the Grants, they were dressed very casually.

"You're doing the talking," Stevie reminded me. "I'm just here to sign the papers."

Stevie kept her head down as she got out of the car and grabbed the carrier in the back seat. I climbed out too, straightening my blue button-down. I approached the Hextons and was met with smiles and friendly nods.

"Oscar Hexton." Oscar shook my hand first. "This is my wife, Ophelia, and my daughter Mara. She's visiting from Atlanta."

"Nice to meet you. I'm Ember, and that's my sister Stevie."

"I've never met a woman with that name before," Ophelia chimed in. She wore an orange top that reminded me of a beach umbrella and round sunglasses.

"It's short for Stevana," Stevie replied. "My pa's name was Steven."

"Then you must be the oldest, being named after your father." Oscar chuckled.

Stevie shrugged, struggling to find a comfortable way to hold Whiskers without handing him over prematurely.

"Let's get started, shall we?" I gestured toward the steps leading to the Grants' front porch, which was bigger than my mom's living room.

The Hextons seemed just as rigid as Stevie when we stood at the front door. Oscar cleared his throat and grabbed his wife's hand. Ophelia eyed the cat carrier and straightened her shoulders. Their daughter Mara, whose outfit was much tamer than her mother's, lifted her chin like she was preparing herself for an onslaught of criticism.

Stevie nudged me, and I realized none of us had actually rung the doorbell.

The front door opened before I had the chance.

Memories raced through my mind as Mrs. Grant opened the door wide and stood in the foyer wearing a pink cocktail dress and heels. Her reddish hair was fiery as ever, and her cheeks were rosy. I couldn't tell if she was upset or if she'd put on too much blush.

"They're here, Earle!" she yelled over her shoulder. "Hello, Ophelia." She pursed her lips. "That's a colorful shirt you have on. I saw one just like it at that little souvenir shop near campus."

"And I'm pretty sure I've seen that dress on one too many girls attending their high school prom," Ophelia retaliated. "I suppose if a woman in her sixties can pull it off, anyone can."

"I don't care if she's a witch," Stevie whispered. "I like her."

"I'm glad y'all could make it," Mrs. Grant continued, keeping a pseudo-smile on her face. "I figured your home might be a little cramped, so I'm happy to host."

"How kind." Ophelia stepped inside first, inching a bit too close to Mrs. Grant as she walked past her. Ophelia was a head taller than her rival.

Oscar and Mara followed after Ophelia, and I got butterflies in my stomach as I imagined what the next two hours would be like. The Hextons had appeared to be friendly, but judging from the scene I'd just witnessed, Ophelia Hexton didn't let Mrs. Grant belittle her one little bit.

"And you two must be..." Mrs. Grant paused, studying me and Stevie.

"Seers," I said. I reached out to shake her hand, but she didn't return the friendly gesture. I quickly moved my hand away from her and slyly tucked a strand of hair behind my ear. I rarely wore it down because the humidity made it frizzy.

"Where's Bonnie and Jenny Mae?" She narrowed her eyes and fixated on Stevie. "I thought they were assigned to Cottonberry. They're lovely ladies. They always bring me scented candles when they come for a visit. The last one was jasmine, and I've already used it all up."

"They weren't available to mediate today," I explained. "We're their replacements."

Stevie held the black carrier in front of her and stayed standing behind me.

"Where are y'all from?" Mrs. Grant stood on her tiptoes to get a better look at Stevie.

"Misty Key." My voice wavered as if I wasn't sure of my answer.

"Oh." Mrs. Grant raised her eyebrows. "I remember you two."

"Yes, we're really—"

"You're those bakery gals who found our family ghoul last year," she interrupted. "You have no idea what a pain it was to conjure a new one."

"My apologies." I clenched my hands into fists. I didn't even know what I was apologizing for. Finding their graveyard ghoul dead? Reporting a fleshbug infestation and preventing innocent people from dying?

"I suppose I have no choice but to cooperate. I just want my Whiskers back." Mrs. Grant stepped aside and held her chin high as the two of us stepped into the foyer and followed the sound of voices.

Stevie huffed as she walked carefully behind me. The Grants' house reminded me of the Crystal

Grande Hotel, except it was much brighter. Most of the furniture in the formal living area was white. A shimmering chandelier hung above the sitting area, giving off the impression that the Grants had a lot of extra spending money.

Mrs. Grant's heels clanged in the hallway. She led us to the study where a large rectangular table had been set up with three chairs on each side and two chairs at the head. Dr. Grant, a man who insisted on being addressed as *Doctor* even though he had no medical degree, stood next to his chair wearing a light-colored suit. It was better than the velvet smoking jacket he'd been wearing during our last visit.

"Please, take a seat everyone." Dr. Grant looked the opposite of his wife—tall and lanky with golden-blond hair. He waited for the Hextons to sit down opposite from him.

Stevie and I took our places at the head of the table.

"OK, let's get started." I stayed standing and pulled the case file from my purse. I set it on the table as Stevie moved her chair up against a wall and farther away from the group. She sat down and rested the carrier in her lap.

"One moment." Mrs. Grant held up her finger. "My son will be right down." Her eyes darted to Stevie.

She'd remembered us just fine, and she'd also remembered that Stevie had dated her son in high school.

"Your son?" I kept an emotionless expression on my face while my stomach churned. I resisted the urge to glance over my shoulder at Stevie because I knew she must be filled with fury on the inside.

"Yes, he's visiting from Birmingham," Mrs. Grant responded.

A figure darkened the doorway. It was a face I hadn't seen since high school and had never thought about much until Stevie had confessed last year that she'd dated him. Warner Grant had reddish hair like his mother and dark eyes like his father. He was of average height, and in high school he would have been considered the snobbish jock type. But as an older man with a wife and kids, he'd lost his immature smirk and six-pack abs.

"Hello, everyone." Warner nodded at the Hextons and took the open seat next to his mother.

I cleared my throat, preparing to glide through the mediation before Mrs. Grant could say anything that might light Stevie's temper on fire.

"Now that we're all here, let's talk about Whiskers," I continued.

"Chewy," Ophelia chimed in. "That's what *we* call him, but y'all can carry on calling him Whiskers."

"Right. As I was saying, let's discuss Whiskers, also known to the Hexton family as Chewy." My mediation skills were a little rusty. I hadn't done one in a long time. "My name is Ember Greene, and behind me is my sister Stevie." I snuck a glimpse of Warner. He didn't even blink at the mention of my sister's name. "We are both licensed Seers assigned to this case by the Clairs."

"Yes, we know all this," Mrs. Grant interrupted.

"Patience, darling," Dr. Grant said. "They have to give us a formal introduction. That's how all of this works."

"Thank you, Dr. Grant." I nodded and glanced down at my notes. "The first thing we're going to do before we dive in is review the rules and agenda for the evening."

"We're prepared to sit here all night," Ophelia added, raising her hand. "Whatever it takes." She shot a devious glare at Mrs. Grant.

"We're *also* prepared to get our little Whiskers back," Mrs. Grant said.

"That's great." I forced a smile. My gut told me we might be in for a long night. Neither lady planned on backing down. "So, the most important rule here is that we allow each party to speak without interruption. Each party also needs to speak calmly without insulting or attacking specific individuals. As it says in the handbook, please refrain from using accusatory statements and instead stick to topics based in facts. Any questions?"

Both groups looked at each other.

"No," Dr. Grant answered.

"OK." I took another deep breath, feeling as if I was in the middle of a business presentation. I repressed memories and thoughts about Mr. Cohen's phone call and pulled myself back to the present. "I'm going to ask each family about their interactions with Whiskers, and why they feel that Whiskers should reside with them. Please, do not interrupt anyone. If anything inappropriate or unfair is said, *I* will intervene."

"Got it," Ophelia muttered.

"After each family tells their side of the story, we will brainstorm together some solutions to the problem," I continued, glancing at the case file periodically so I didn't miss a step. "Once we settle on a solution, we will all agree to it in writing. I will be taking notes along the way so that no detail is left undiscussed. You are all welcome to take notes as well. Does everyone agree with this process?"

I looked at the Hextons first and then at the Grants. I clasped my hands together; my palms were sweaty. I studied the look on Warner's face as his eyes darted around the room. I still wasn't sure if he'd recognized me and Stevie. But one thing was almost certain in my mind.

He didn't really resemble my nephew, Orion.

"I agree." Dr. Grant nodded.

"So do we," Oscar added.

"Wonderful." I sat down and adjusted my blouse. "Who would like to start?" I looked at the Grants since they'd lived in Cottonberry the longest.

"Yes, I will go first." Mrs. Grant spoke up and rose to her feet at the same time.

"You don't have to stand," I said.

She slowly sat back down, retaining her cavalier expression.

"Our ancestors grew up here in Cottonberry," she stated. "We've had countless familiars show up on our doorstep when the timing was right and serve us well. Whiskers is no different."

"When did he first arrive?" I asked, jotting down a few notes.

Mrs. Grant's eyes darted to the carrier on Stevie's lap.

"Last summer," she answered, looking to her husband for support. He nodded.

"Yes," he agreed. "July, I believe."

"Yes, we had a death in the family." Mrs. Grant looked down, and when she focused on the mediation again her eyes were glossy. "My cousin's hairdresser's neighbor passed away suddenly." A soft giggle escaped Ophelia's lips. "You have a problem with that, Ophelia?"

Her solemn expression left her face immediately, and Warner wrapped his arm around her to keep her from raising her voice.

"I didn't say anything, Pamela."

I hadn't heard Mrs. Grant's first name in so long I'd almost forgotten it.

"But you laughed," she argued. "You opened your mouth and noise came out, which isn't allowed."

"*Mom*," Warner muttered.

Mrs. Grant crossed her arms. "She thinks it's funny, Earle." She pointed at Ophelia, demonstrating the exact opposite sort of behavior than should be displayed during a mediation. "She thinks it's funny that the poor woman my cousin's hairdresser had the privilege of knowing just dropped dead after choking on piece of tenderloin. I've had to become vegetarian because of it."

"Calm down, dear," Dr. Grant instructed her.

"Oh? Then why did you serve deviled crab dip at last month's Magical Mingle?" Ophelia asked.

"Seafood and red meat are *very* different, Ophelia, and you know it!" Mrs. Grant's rosy cheeks turned even more scarlet.

"Ladies, please," I interjected. The two of them were almost as bad as Aqua and Stevie fighting over the last peach Danish. "Mrs. Grant, please continue."

"Whiskers showed up on our doorstep during a difficult time." She avoided making eye contact with any of the Hextons. "I knew it was meant to be."

"OK." I looked at the Hextons. "Who would like to represent the Hextons' side of this dispute?"

"I will." Ophelia leaned forward in her chair. "We moved to Cottonberry last month after some trouble with some of our non-magical neighbors. We were welcomed into the witching community here with open arms, and then Chewy, I mean *Whiskers*, just appeared in my kitchen one day."

Mrs. Grant cleared her throat.

"It's true," her daughter Mara chimed in. "I was visiting that weekend. My mother was making her famous chicken and dumplings, and there he was. It was like he appeared out of thin air."

"And that's when you noticed that Whiskers was missing?" I asked, looking at the Grants.

"That's right," Mrs. Grant confirmed. "It wasn't until I came over with a lemon Bundt cake that I noticed our sweet baby had been kidnapped. Of course, I reported it immediately."

"Why would I have let Chewy, I mean *Whiskers*, gallivant around the house if I'd kidnapped him?" Ophelia scowled. "How stupid do you think I am?"

"Well—"

"It was a hypothetical question, Pamela," Ophelia snapped at her. "You don't even know for sure that Whiskers and Chewy are the same cat."

"I showed you the scar on his paw," Mrs. Grant responded, raising her voice. "A scar like that doesn't just show up at random."

"All right." I held up my hands. "If you two don't cut this out, I'm going to need a megaphone."

Warner chuckled—something I hadn't expected.

"She's right," Oscar said plainly. "Let's stick to the rules, folks."

"Thank you." I exhaled loudly and took a few notes. "So, let me get this straight. Whiskers appeared to the Grant family last summer, and he also appeared to the Hexton family last month. And we know that this is the same black cat in question because of a scar on his paw?"

"That is correct," Dr. Grant agreed.

Oscar nodded on behalf of his family.

"Might I point out that the Grants have a specific need for a familiar at the moment and—" Mrs. Grant frowned when Ophelia cut her off.

"The Hextons are *also* in need of a familiar," Ophelia added.

"One at a time, please," I said.

"I propose that we perform a winnowing." As soon as Mrs. Grant made her suggestion, the room fell silent. I glanced over my shoulder at Stevie. She shrugged.

"What's a winnowing?"

"It's a ceremony," Dr. Grant explained. "It's used to communicate with familiars, specifically, to link them to a witching family. If we perform one, Whiskers will be magically tied to one of our families, and the results are absolute."

"How exactly does that happen?" I asked.

"Basically a spell will be cast, and Whiskers will have full comprehension of the situation at hand for about thirty minutes," Mara said. "He'll understand that he needs to choose a family, and then he'll pick one of us. The results of an official winnowing are enforced by magic."

"So, he'll choose, and then that's it?" I wrote down the suggestion in my notes. It was the same thing I'd attempted with Aqua, but in a way that used magic.

"Correct," Dr. Grant responded.

"Does anyone have any other ideas as to how we can resolve this matter fairly?" I looked from the Grants to the Hextons.

After a few minutes of silence, I made eye contact with Stevie. A winnowing was our best chance at finishing the mediation early and getting back to Misty Key. I flipped through the case file in front of me.

"Shall I get the rose oil?" Mrs. Grant spoke up.

* * *

The study had been rearranged so there was open space in the center of the room.

Stevie had silently removed Whiskers from his carrier, averting her eyes from Warner any time he came close. Mrs. Grant had retrieved her rose oil, and the group had agreed that Mara would recite the spell. Both families had officially agreed to perform the ceremony and honor the results.

My heart pounded as I double-checked the scar on Whiskers's paw.

"Good luck, little guy," I whispered. "Pretty soon you'll understand what's going on here. Choose wisely."

Stevie walked to the center of the study. The Grants and the Hextons stood at opposite ends of the room. Mrs. Grant stepped forward and dabbed each of the cat's paws with rose oil. She returned to her post, and Stevie carefully placed Whiskers in the middle of the room. He stayed still, glancing at all of us curiously.

"Once I say the spell, everyone needs to remain silent so he can make his decision," Mara said.

The shades had been drawn, and Mrs. Grant had dimmed the lights. Minus the tension between the Grants and the Hextons, the study resonated serene vibes. I was sure Whiskers would have the calm environment he needed to make a choice. Letting him be in charge of his own destiny seemed like the best decision anyway.

Stevie and I stepped back, leaning our backs against a wall as Mara recited her spell. A mysterious breeze engulfed the room as she held out her wand and pointed it at Whiskers. Tingles moved up and down my spine as I watched Whiskers look around the room with a humanlike expression.

He looked at the Grants, and then he looked at the Hextons.

He obviously knew what he had to do.

A few minutes passed. I wasn't sure if waiting was normal or if it was all part of the process. I didn't want to break the silence and ask. Mrs. Grant stood on her tiptoes staring at Whiskers as intensely as she could while Ophelia shook her head with disapproval. Dr. Grant covered his wife's mouth to stop her from calling out to him. But he moved his hand when Whiskers began moving in their direction.

Mrs. Grant was seconds away from singing her victory to the entire neighborhood, but Whiskers stopped.

Whiskers turned back to the Hextons and took a few steps. Ophelia's eyes went wide as she watched him, covering her mouth to stop herself from ruining the moment. A giant smile spread across Oscar's face as he gently nudged his daughter.

I raised my eyebrows. The thoughts running through Whiskers's mind were beyond me.

My stomach leaped when Whiskers stopped again.

Great. Even Whiskers can't figure this one out.

Whiskers turned and looked at me as if he could hear my thoughts. I looked at Stevie but she seemed just as clueless. My heart pounded as Whiskers trotted toward me, jumping up onto a nearby table that had been pushed out of the way, and finally hopping into my arms.

He'd chosen *me*.

The mysterious breeze in the room circled the two of us before disappearing.

My eyes went wider than powdered donut holes.

The sound of Mrs. Grant stamping her high heels on the floor stole my attention. She shoved her husband and son out of the way and pointed right at me.

"Cheater!" she shouted.

Chapter 8

"The results of a winnowing are final, what can I say?"
Nova spoke plainly on the other end of the phone, but I
still had a hard time comprehending what had just
happened.

Stevie and I had been kicked out of the Grants'
home. Again. If this hadn't solidified Mrs. Grant's
distaste for psychics, then I didn't know what would. I
was the new owner of a witch's familiar—a black cat I
knew nothing about—and I was pretty sure I would
never be allowed back in Cottonberry ever again.

For Stevie, I was sure that was a good thing.

"But I'm not a witch," I responded, gripping my
cell phone even tighter.

"You are sometimes," Stevie muttered from a
corner of our hotel room.

"Can't they perform the ceremony again?" I
glanced at Whiskers. He sat quietly on the bed
watching my heated conversation.

"No," Nova answered. "You'll have to keep him
around until he's served his purpose and moves on to
another...um, family." She cleared her throat.

"You were going to say *witching* family." I
shook my head. "Look, Whiskers or Chewy or whatever
his actual name is isn't the problem. I now have two
very unhappy covens and no signatures saying that

this case has been peacefully resolved. What are we supposed to do?"

"They agreed to the winnowing, so they have to sign," Nova explained. "If they refuse, we'll have to send a form to Wisteria, Inc. and let them deal with it."

"OK." I took a deep breath. I was out of arguments. "Fine. We'll leave in the morning as planned, and if anything changes—"

"I'll give you a call," Nova finished. "Remember, everything happens for a reason, Ember. Whiskers choosing to go back to the bakery with you wasn't an accident."

"Tell that to Mrs. Grant when she sics the family ghoul on us," I commented.

I hung up the phone, my eyes darting around the room as I wondered where to sit. Stevie occupied the only chair, and the hotel had messed up my reservation and given us a room with one king bed instead of two queens. No other rooms were available.

Whiskers stretched, tapping his paw on the comforter, which happened to be a beachy pattern made up of palm trees and flamingos.

"I'm sure the Grants are hatching a plan as we speak," Stevie said. She skimmed through the list of local TV channels and tossed it on the bedside table.

"I'm sorry about Warner," I said as I carefully sat on an unoccupied corner of the bed. Whiskers didn't move.

"Don't be. That loser didn't even recognize me, so it's all fine." She forced a smile. I had an inkling that part of her had been a little disappointed but the other part had just faced her fear of seeing him again.

"I'm sure we're the topic of conversation this evening." I grabbed the hair tie around my wrist and ran my fingers through my hair. "I'm never agreeing to a winnowing again. But at least the Hextons seemed nice about it."

"That's because the Hextons are normal," Stevie pointed out. "The Grants live in a fantasy world."

I observed the way Whiskers rested in the center of our conversation. He seemed more relaxed. He hadn't searched for a hiding place when we'd entered our hotel room, and he hadn't glared at me for flushing the toilet or using the sink. He hadn't been a fan of the loud noises in the past. Although I still hoped he would start eating once we made it back to Misty Key.

"If Yogi doesn't mind him, then he can't be so bad, right?" I shrugged. Looking for the positives of our situation was the only tactic I hadn't tried yet.

"That's true," Stevie admitted. "He hasn't tried to chew him up and spit him out. But do we have to keep on calling him Whiskers?"

"Do you have another name in mind?" I asked her.

Stevie stared at Whiskers, leaning forward. "Do you even like that name, bud?" She sat back and wrinkled her nose. "Who even came up with that name? *Whiskers*. It reminds me of an old man smoking a pipe."

"Though not as old and overweight as our friend Warner," I joked, hoping to brighten the atmosphere. Especially since I had to share a bed with Stevie, and I didn't want her to push me out of it in the middle of the night like she'd done many times when we were kids.

"He did look older, didn't he?" Stevie cracked a subtle smile. "It's weird seeing people you haven't seen in years. I still see the same old Warner from high school, but it's like he's been planted in a different body or something. I wonder if people think the same about us?"

"We're not *that* old. Now you sound like Aqua."

"Everything's old to Aqua," Stevie responded. "Why do you think she switches cell phones every six months?"

"She texts so much that her screen stops working?"

"Heaven forbid," Stevie muttered. A slight chuckle escaped her lips.

I grinned and glanced at the time. Before I knew it, I'd be back on the road.

And moving on to my next problem—the fate of our family bakery.

A knock on the door disturbed my thoughts. My pulse quickened as I glanced at Stevie. Neither of us had been expecting company. I slowly walked toward the door and opened it. My mind ran through hundreds of scenarios, the primary one being Mrs. Grant devising an evil plan to get Whiskers back.

I might not have been wrong.

"Warner?" I raised my eyebrows, all of my thoughts now on Stevie's temper. "What are you doing here?"

"I'm sorry," he said, looking behind me at Stevie. He'd changed into a college T-shirt that fit just a little too snug around his torso, and there were beads of sweat on his brow. "Y'all left before I had to chance to..." He clenched his jaw.

"Please inform your mother that I'm doing everything I can to sort this out. I've found loopholes before, and I'm sure I can—"

"No," he stopped me. "I mean, my mother has been ranting all night, but I'm not here to talk about that."

"Then why?"

"Stevie." His expression softened even more when he said her name.

"I have nothing to say to you," she responded, joining me at the door. She tried to push it shut, but Warner wouldn't let her. Apparently, he still had the strength of a man who'd spent years lifting weights and playing football. He just didn't look it.

"You have every reason to hate me," he pleaded. "But when I saw you at my parents' house...well, all of that guilt came back."

"And I hope it eats away at you until the day you die," Stevie coldly responded.

"Look." He wiped away a trickle of sweat. "Can I talk to you in private? I have some things I need to say."

"You expect me to believe you've grown a conscience?" Stevie took a step back and balled her hands into fists.

"A wife and three kids can do that to you," he said.

"Whatever you have to say to me, you can say it right here in front of my sister." She took a deep breath and crossed her arms.

"OK." He gulped. "Stevie, I'm sorry about what happened."

"Oh, you're *sorry*." Her voice was eerily calm, and it gave me goose bumps. I knew it was just a matter of time before I'd be witnessing a volcanic eruption. I was terrified, but at the same time, I was hooked.

"Stevie," I calmly whispered.

"You destroyed my life, Warner. *Sorry* ain't gonna cut it." She bit the corner of her lip, her eyes glossy. "I have a son. He's ten. And thanks to you, he will *never* know his father. Do you have any idea how hard it is for me to look in the mirror every day?"

"A son?" Warner's eyes went wide and most of the color left his cheeks. "Stevie, I had no idea."

"Get lost before I do something I'll regret." A tear ran down her cheek, but her expression wasn't sorrowful. She glared at Warner in a way I'd never seen her do before—with a deep disdain for everyone and everything he touched in this world.

"Let me help you. Let me try and make things right."

"It's too late," she shouted. She rubbed the tears from her cheeks and took a few steps toward Warner with a glimmer of hatred in her eyes. It was enough for him to back up against the wall in the hallway. "You're still the same old Warner—spoiled and selfish. I never want to see you again."

"But your son—"

"Don't you dare say a word about him! Now, get lost!" Stevie was almost screaming by now.

My heart raced, and I looked up and down the hallway, expecting a few other guests to open their doors and complain about the noise.

Warner nodded and scurried toward the nearest elevator.

I followed Stevie back inside our hotel room and quickly shut the door.

An odd silence passed over us.

"Are you OK?" I waited for her response. An explanation. Anything that might finally solve the mystery as to who my nephew's father was.

After a few minutes, Stevie glared at me too.

"No, I'm not OK. I've spent over ten years trying to forget about that man, and you insisted on dragging me here. I'm sick of ripping off scabs. This is *your* fault."

"*My* fault?" I couldn't help but defend myself even though I was scared of what Stevie might say to me next. She knew my secrets, and she knew what to say to make me hurt just as much as she was. "How was I supposed to know Warner would be here? You think I planned this?"

"You could have come alone," she argued. "You could have found me a temporary replacement. You could have found a loophole like you claim you're so good at. But no. You had to do things *your* way. New budget. New prices. The baking classes. Things always have to be done your way."

"Is this about Warner or the bakery?" My chest went tight.

"Both," she yelled. "It's about how you always think you know best, and then you screw up everything!"

"At least I bother speaking my mind," I shouted back. "I never know what's going on with you, let alone your issues with Warner Grant. I guess not even your sister is good enough to know the truth." I knew she was upset, which made the rest of her worries spill out. It was easy to blame other people when things went wrong. I found myself doing it time and time again. But her words still stung.

"You have no idea what you're talking about, Ember!"

"And I probably never will, because you won't let me." I sniffled, and a pressure built up behind my eyes. "I came back to Misty Key to try and fix things that were broken. It would have been nice to know that some things prefer to stay that way."

"So, that's it, huh?" Stevie inched toward the bathroom door. "You think you're better than me."

"I would at least acknowledge the father of my child," I blurted out. My words were hasty.

A tear ran down Stevie's face, and I immediately felt sick to my stomach.

"Warner is *not* the father," she responded.

"Stevie, I didn't mean to—"

"Orion's father is dead." She slammed the bathroom door shut.

Maybe me taking that job offer and leaving Misty Key would be the best thing for everyone.

Chapter 9

Stevie hadn't spoken a word to me all day.

Our car ride back to Misty Key had been uncomfortably silent, and I'd preferred it that way. I didn't want to say anything else to her out of frustration. Orion's father was dead, and I'd reopened Stevie's wound. It wasn't something I'd done on purpose, and I regretted the things I'd said.

But I didn't regret the changes I'd made to the Lunar Bakery.

Those changes were needed to keep the business out of the red.

Now back at the bakery, Stevie was stuck in the kitchen filling special orders, and Luann had called in sick. I helped Aqua with the rush of afternoon java-seekers and tried as hard as I could to bury myself in work until closing time. I took orders quickly. I made the coffees, and I'd even scheduled in time to clean the floors.

The bell above the bakery door chimed, and my heart pounded.

I hadn't seen Thad in a while. He'd been busy working extra shifts at the Crystal Grande alongside his uncle and mentor, Louie Stone. Not only was Louie the groundskeeper and head of maintenance, he was also chief of the clan of shifters that lived near the swamps. They were of the wolf variety, and they'd adopted Thad into their group last year when he'd wandered south looking for answers about his cloudy past.

There were days when Thad looked more wolf-like than manly with wild hair, a scruffy beard, and muscles that guaranteed he could sprint through the wilderness for days. But other days, he looked more like himself. Thad had finally gotten a haircut. His dark locks were gelled, and he was clean-shaven like he'd been the first time we'd met.

Thad walked to the front counter, and Aqua dashed to take his order. She twirled the end of her braid and sported a playful smile like she did any time a man stood in front of her. Thad's eyes darted around the bakery until they met mine. I crossed my arms and watched Aqua read him our afternoon specials. Thad ordered an iced coffee and our last chocolate croissant.

"I like the new look," I commented as he took a step back from the register.

"I've been sleeping," he answered, placing his hands in his jean pockets. "It's amazing what a simple noise machine will do."

"Are you staying or will you be needing a *doggy* bag?" Aqua chimed in, giggling at her own joke.

"And there it is," he muttered, directing his grin at Aqua. She blushed. "Got to love that Greene family humor."

"We are dog lovers," I added. I paused, wishing I would have taken the time to think about my response before blurting out the words. I'd said one embarrassing thing after another in front of him and couldn't seem to break the habit. The worst was when he'd visited me in the hospital last month, and I'd been under the influence of pain medication.

Aqua giggled some more.

"How's the new neighbor? Silent as the grave?" Thad carried on with our conversation. Had he read into what I'd said? I never knew with Thad. Unless I was conducting a psychic reading, his thoughts and feelings about everything remained a mystery to me.

"Funny." I raised my eyebrows. I hadn't seen our new neighbor Junior in a while. He'd been back and forth between Misty Key and Chattanooga for weeks.

"He's been really busy," Aqua chimed in, setting Thad's order on the counter. She'd opted for the doggy bag anyway for the chocolate croissant. "We hardly notice when he's home."

"And how are things here at the bakery?" he asked.

"Fine." I tilted my head. "Where are you going with all of this?"

"Do I need a reason to visit the best café in town?" He shrugged. The fabric of his thin T-shirt clung to his chest, revealing a hint of what was hidden underneath—the solid muscle of an ex-Marine.

I pulled my eyes away from him and re-focused on the matter at hand. "I guess you've seen the papers."

"I have," he answered. "George Carmichael is finally rescued, according to the papers, and then he dies anyway days later. Horrible luck, right?" He narrowed his eyes and studied me. The heat of his glare made my pulse quicken. I took a deep breath to try and steady it. "What?"

"Huh?" I cleared my throat.

"There's more to the story, isn't there?" He cocked an eyebrow as if it was my duty to fill him in. "Don't tell me it was a magical mistake."

"She's like a magnet for trouble," Aqua said as she wiped the glass pastry case and eyed the empty café tables. "Haven't you figured that out by now?"

"Yes, thank you, Aqua, for your input." I grabbed my broom and busied myself with unnecessary chores.

"What happened?" Thad patiently watched me sweep the area near the front entrance. He carefully took the broom from my hands and pulled me to a secluded table—the one in a quiet corner where Nova always sat when she came to talk. "Ember, what's going on?"

I wanted to tell him everything, but I didn't want to burden him with my problems.

He had enough of his own.

"It's nothing." I rubbed my forehead. "Just Seer business and boring stuff like that."

And also, my sister hated me and we were at risk of losing the family business because of a red velvet cheesecake.

"I'm not leaving until you fess up," he said. The deep tone of his voice yanked me back to all of the times he'd shown up when I'd needed him the most. If my family turned their backs on me, Thad might be my only friend left in Misty Key apart from Rickiah.

"Will you accept a sob story about our latest shipment of produce? The sorry state of those lemons would make anyone's face turn sour."

"Hey, I'm playing by your rules here." He folded his arms and gripped his biceps. "You never let *me* get away with it, so I'm not going to let you keep your problems bottled up. We're friends, aren't we?"

My eyes fixated on his pupils and then on the dark circles that outlined each iris. An inviting shade of hickory. Thad and I had never addressed our relationship, mostly because there was nothing to address. Half of the time, I wasn't even sure how long he planned on staying in Misty Key.

"If I say yes, do you promise never to tell anyone what I said to you that day in the hospital?"

"You mean—"

"Don't say it," I cut him off. "I don't need fragments of my mistakes floating off into the universe." I drummed my fingers on the table. "George Carmichael was murdered."

"He's rich." Thad placed his elbows on the table and leaned in close. "I'm sure he pissed off lots of people. Dangerous people."

"Dangerous people who are fond of red velvet cheesecakes?" I rubbed my temples, doing what I could to stop the panic from setting in. I still had time to get to the bottom of it. I still had time to figure out how a specialty dessert ended up in Room 111.

"Cheesecake?"

"The police found a cheesecake at the scene of the crime," I explained, lowering my voice to almost a whisper. "It was one of ours. Detective Winter thinks it might've killed George Carmichael."

"Was he lactose intolerant?"

"The cheesecake might have been poisoned." I smiled slightly. "If it was, then that's bad news for the bakery."

"So, just trace the cake back to the customer." Thad nodded, satisfied with his solution.

"If it was that easy, the case probably would have been solved by now. The only red velvet cheesecakes that have left this bakery were made by students. Stevie started teaching baking classes this month."

"I see," he responded lowly. "Someone in the class is guilty."

"And we haven't had time to track down all of the cheesecakes because—"

"Out!" The door to the kitchen flung open as Stevie shouted.

Whiskers came trotting into the café.

I rolled my eyes.

That cat was the definition of clingy. He'd followed me and Stevie everywhere the moment we'd gotten back to Misty Key. Despite our efforts, he'd somehow found a way out of the house and tracked us to the bakery too. He'd been napping in my office alongside Yogi all morning. At least, that's what I'd thought.

"Come here, little guy," Aqua cooed. She loved animals, but I knew she was also frustrated she hadn't established a connection with Whiskers. Not one strong enough to read his thoughts anyway.

"What's a cat doing in the kitchen?" Thad sniffed the air and watched Aqua as she petted the black fur ball and then picked him up.

"Meet Whiskers, our new family pet." I gestured toward him. "Because we don't have enough to do around here already." I sighed. "It's a long story."

"As is the complicated murder of George Carmichael," he muttered. "Well, I can't solve your problems, but I sure as hell can help."

"How?" I drummed my fingers on the table some more.

"Come to the hotel with me tomorrow night," he replied.

"I'm sorry...what?" I couldn't help but envision the two of us hand in hand in the lobby of the Crystal Grande. Butterflies whizzed around in my stomach. I hadn't gotten that sort of attention from a man in a long time.

"The Mardi Gras kick-off party," he clarified. "Come with me tomorrow night. It's the perfect opportunity to snoop around."

"Oh, of course." I exhaled loudly, remembering the town's upcoming celebration that was sure to pile even more work onto my plate as more tourists began arriving for the occasion. "Um..."

"You were planning on going, right? The whole town is going to be there."

"The whole town minus Mary Jean and the do-gooders." I took a deep breath and pulled my mind back to the investigation. I had a lot of students left to visit, and Stevie hadn't had the chance yet to try and connect with Mr. Carmichael's ghost. The Mardi Gras party might be the perfect opportunity.

"Ems, you have to go." Aqua joined our conversation, still rubbing Whiskers's shiny coat. "You and Stevie need to get out and have some fun."

"And the murder investigation?" I glanced in her direction. She didn't know I wasn't the one who needed convincing. I was pretty sure it pained Stevie to even be in the same building as me after the things I'd said to her.

"If something else is going down, it'll happen this weekend. At the hotel." Aqua smiled at Thad. "Thad's right. It'll be the perfect opportunity to sleuth or whatever it is you do. Thad can be your date."

My stomach churned as she uttered the word *date*.

The last date I'd been on, I'd been dumped.

"Call it whatever you want, but Stevie is the one who needs to jump on that train." I avoided making eye contact with Thad. "Her best chance of speaking to our dead friend Mr. Carmichael will be at the Crystal Grande."

"Stevie!"

Aqua's sudden shouting made me flinch.

Whiskers wiggled out of her grasp and jumped on my lap.

Stevie huffed as she stepped into the café wearing an apron splotched with flour. Her midnight hair was pinned back, and there were bags under her eyes. She didn't smile, but she didn't frown either. Probably because Thad was in the room.

"You rang?" she said through her teeth. "I'm very busy, Aqua. This had better be good. And keep that cat out of here. He keeps sniffing around my ingredients."

"We were just talking about the Mardi Gras party tomorrow night," Aqua continued. "We're all going. You included."

"Aqua, I—"

"The bakery will be closed by then," she went on. "Mom will watch Orion. You have some dead people to talk to."

Stevie took a deep breath, looking at everyone in the room but me.

She nodded. "Yeah, OK. Fine. I'll go."

She turned around and went back into the kitchen without so much as a *hello* for Thad.

"She's always ornery when she gets gluten-free cupcake orders." Aqua pulled one of our usual excuses for my sister's rude behavior out of the pile. "Oh, and she skipped her espresso this morning."

Thad studied me for a minute before accepting Aqua's excuses. His canine half sensed emotions much like a family dog.

"Sure." He narrowed his eyes. "I guess I'll see you ladies tomorrow night."

"Yep." I grinned, but Thad's stare seemed to pierce right through me.

"Until tomorrow, Ember."

Thad left the bakery, and immediately I closed my eyes, hating that I had nothing in my wardrobe for the occasion. It didn't matter. I was going to the party to take care of business and nothing else. It didn't matter what I looked like.

But part of me still cared.

"I have something I need to say," Aqua stated.

I rolled my eyes. "If this is about me and Thad, save it. Your dating advice is the worst."

"I'm talking about you and Stevie." She placed a hand on her hip.

The bell above the door chimed and more customers filed in.

"What do you mean?"

"I mean, I'm not an idiot, despite what you two might think," she whispered. "Something happened in Cottonberry, and I suggest you fix it before things get even more awkward around here."

Aqua darted back to the register and smiled wide.

I looked down at Whiskers, and he stared back at me.

"Finding the killer would be easier," I muttered.

Chapter 10

"You're not the only one with something to lose here."

Stevie jumped in the passenger's seat and wrinkled her nose when she saw Whiskers in the back of my car. I bit the side of my lip and began the drive to the older part of town where Zinny Pellman was waiting for me. I'd called her office and found out she'd been working from home all week.

"He insisted on coming," I stated. It was true. No matter where I left Whiskers, he always found his way back to me.

"And Yogi?"

"At home napping as usual," I replied. "He doesn't seem to care that Whiskers has been following me everywhere."

"What's your problem, huh?" Stevie said, looking toward the backseat before checking her reflection in the rearview mirror. "I bet he's a little spy employed by Wisteria, Inc. You watch. This is all some kind of setup."

"I don't see why they would target us," I said, staring straight ahead as I passed by Main Street and drove further away from the beach. "Unless they're wanting buttercream recipes and baking advice. Oh, well. At least he's eating now, so no one can blame us if he drops dead."

"Whatever." She sighed. "We need to get on with our investigation, and I'm not letting you do it alone. The reasons why should be obvious."

They were. Stevie didn't trust me.

We pulled up to Zinny's residence as the sky began to darken. I had two objectives: to learn what the *Misty Messenger* knew about George Carmichael and to see Zinny's red velvet cheesecake for myself. I walked up to the front door with Stevie, Whiskers lurking behind us.

A light was on in the living room. Whiskers batted his paw at a rogue weed near the porch. Zinny's yard had grown wild, standing out from all of her neighbors'. Her bright door needed a new coat of paint, and the cracks in the concrete looked like they'd been there since I was a child. It was very possible that they had.

Stevie knocked on the door and flicked a mosquito hovering near her shoulder. The humidity had seemed worse than usual all day, and the evening was no exception. Pretty soon the night's silence would be hijacked by the chirping of thousands of crickets. Zinny's overgrown grass didn't help the problem.

Zinny answered the door, her eyes darting to our hands. She wiped the smirk from her face.

"You didn't bring me anything?" She abandoned the front door and moved at the pace of a snail toward the kitchen. Her gray hair was matted, and her petite frame looked rounder than ever in her knit cardigan. Whiskers dashed inside after her.

Stevie waltzed into the kitchen, where a microwave dinner sat on the counter along with potato chip crumbs and a half-eaten package of sandwich cookies. Zinny made her way to the family room and sat in an armchair across from the TV.

"I think you have enough sweets," Stevie commented.

Zinny rubbed her eyes and squinted in Stevie's direction.

"I know why you're here," she said. "You're here about the Carmichael murder."

Stevie and I exchanged wary looks.

"I can't pop in and visit my favorite student?" Stevie chuckled.

"You forget that I have sources in the police department," Zinny replied. "I know about the trouble you're in. In fact, some might say I know too much." She looked toward the fridge. "Go ahead. My red velvet cheesecake is safe and sound. That detective stopped by yesterday and asked me about it."

I cautiously opened the fridge.

Whiskers scanned the contents.

The red velvet cheesecake sat on the top shelf, and most of it had been eaten. I nodded at Stevie. Zinny's cheesecake wasn't to blame. Zinny cleared her throat and stared at the wall in front of her.

"Zinny, what do you know about the case?" I asked her.

She looked down at the beige carpet underneath her feet.

"I don't think it's a good idea for you two to get mixed up in this," she answered, lowering her voice. Her eyes closed for a moment and then opened again. Stevie and I both moved toward her. It wasn't like Zinny to be so quiet, especially when she had the inside scoop.

"Why?" Stevie tilted her head and studied the family room. Whiskers sniffed around the room like Yogi normally did.

"The Carmichaels are powerful people," she continued. "Much too powerful for little old me to handle. My hands are tied." Her eyes closed again, but for a longer period of time. When she opened them, my stomach started twisting itself into knots. I knew something was wrong.

"You're leaving something out, Zinny," I stated. "What is it? What did you find out?"

"If she's not talking it's because someone paid her not to," Stevie muttered.

"Or threatened her," I added.

Zinny closed her eyes, hardly paying attention to our conversation.

"Zinny." I snapped my fingers. "Zinny!"

Her eyes shot open.

"What aren't you supposed to tell us?" Stevie placed her hands on her hips. "Who paid you to keep your mouth shut?"

"Or threatened you," I added, holding up a finger.

But Zinny wasn't listening. Her eyes had closed again. Her shoulders sank forward, causing her entire body to slip out of her chair and onto the floor. Whiskers meowed uncontrollably, and I immediately knelt next to Zinny and shook her shoulders.

She didn't respond.

"I see her breathing." Stevie nervously scratched the side of her head as I tried again to wake Zinny up. "Give her a nice little smack in the face."

I took a deep breath, my chest so tight it started to burn.

"Are you crazy? Zinny! Zinny, wake up!"

"I'll do it then." Stevie walked forward and didn't hesitate. Her hand hit Zinny's cheek and left a distinct red mark.

Zinny didn't even flinch.

I checked her pulse. Luckily, she still had one, but I wasn't sure for how long.

"Call an ambulance," I instructed.

Stevie had already dialed 911.

All we could do was wait.

* * *

I clutched a box of glazed donuts. They were a tester batch Stevie had made in the wee hours of the morning. Friday had arrived all too quickly and we'd spent Thursday night speculating about Zinny Pellman's condition. An ambulance had taken her to the only hospital in Misty Key, where she'd been kept overnight. Stevie and I didn't know much more.

But we did know that she was awake and breathing.

The two of us walked toward her room, and all at once the smell of rubbing alcohol and industrial-strength cleaner filled my nose. It was one of the many things I hated about hospitals, along with the sterile, white walls and the numbers. Numbers jumped out at me from each and every direction—all of them delivering bad news that weighed on my chest like I was stuck doing bench presses in the gym for eternity. I kept my head down as Stevie knocked on the door and slowly stepped inside.

Zinny was awake and staring at the ceiling. A half-eaten breakfast tray of oatmeal and eggs was next to her. I scrunched my nose. The oatmeal looked bland, and I couldn't imagine it tasted very good. Zinny gave me her full attention when she saw the box in my hands bearing the bakery's logo.

"If the nurses see that they'll take it away," Zinny commented, her voice hoarse and raspy. "It's contraband around here."

"We decided to stop by and make sure you're OK," Stevie said. She'd left Aqua and Luann with a long list of rules and restrictions, even though we only planned on being gone for thirty minutes. Stevie twiddled her fingers as she scanned the tiny recovery room. My guess was that her mind was still back at the bakery, and I was surprised she hadn't called Aqua yet to make sure she hadn't burned the place down.

Memories of Zinny slipping out of her chair into a motionless heap of flesh on the floor flashed in my mind. I shuddered to think what would have happened if we hadn't showed up when we did. Or at all. I could have been standing in a Misty Key cemetery or even the morgue.

"No, you didn't." Zinny chuckled, staring up at the ceiling again. "You came here to see if I changed my mind."

"Don't be silly." Stevie took a step forward, flashing the friendliest expression she could—the one she saved for customers at the bakery.

"You want details about the Carmichael case," she continued. "That much I do remember."

"Let me guess." Stevie shook her head. "You're not going to tell us anything, even though we saved your life."

"Saved my life?" Zinny scoffed. "What happened to me was my own darn fault. The doctors say it was a diabetic coma."

Stevie turned and eyed the box of donuts. I casually hid them behind my back. I couldn't in good conscience let her have them anymore.

"We called an ambulance," I pointed out. "I doubt you would have been able to do that in the state you were in."

"Fine. I'm grateful." She brushed a strand of gray hair out of her eyes. It was even more matted than usual, and it had lost some of its shine. "But that bakery of yours is a health hazard. All of that sugar should come with a warning. Consumers may die of hyperglycemia."

"I'm not the one shoving sweets down your throat." Stevie's cheeks went red.

"OK." I handed Stevie the box of donuts and stepped in front of her. "We're not here to argue with you."

"Or plan a sugar-free menu," Stevie murmured.

"Yes, we came here to make sure you're OK," I firmly stated. "But we also came here because of the bakery. Our business is just as important to this town as the *Misty Messenger*." I cleared my throat and lifted my chin. Zinny had to know I meant business and that I wasn't interested in playing any games with her. "You have some information about the murder case. You can tell us, or you can keep your mouth shut. Although I hate to think what folks around here might say if they ever found out that their beloved and trusted newspaper accepts bribes."

Zinny's low chuckle turned into a cough. "You two are more dangerous than you look."

"We have just as much to lose as you do," I added.

In my heart, I knew it was more. Because losing the bakery was only step one for me. Stevie would resent me for it, my mom would fall into a depression from losing the only thing she had left tying her to her late husband, and I would most likely take Mr. Cohen up on his job offer.

I was at risk of losing my whole family.

"You drive a hard bargain," Zinny replied. She coughed again. "And you're right. I've worked at the *Misty Messenger* for over thirty years and have never accepted money for my silence. It would be a pity to end my career that way."

Stevie and I looked at each other.

"You mean—"

"Yes, my dears," she cut me off. "I was hoping your baking course would help me out with the boredom. The newspaper is closing its doors, and I'm heading into an early retirement."

"Closing?" Stevie chimed in. "But everyone in Misty Key reads the paper. Ma can't drink her morning sweet tea without it."

"Don't be silly. Circulation has been declining for the past ten years. We're out of money. I'm lucky if my next paycheck doesn't bounce." Zinny's eyes darted to the bland oatmeal beside her and she frowned. "I was already doing the jobs of ten employees."

"I'm sorry to hear that," I said.

"Not as sorry as I am." She quietly glanced off into the distance before poking a piece of scrambled egg. "Cold. Cold and disgusting. I suppose my life is doomed to be just as boring as the meals they make me eat." She searched for the box of donuts. "I want one last hoorah, and then I'll tell you what you want to know."

Stevie studied the box in her hands. "I don't want to be sued."

"Honey, if it comes to that I'll be dead anyway." Zinny lunged toward her as best she could and snatched the box of breakfast sweets. "Trust me. That bowl of oatmeal is worse than being dead."

"It's your funeral," Stevie muttered.

Zinny's eyes darted to the door as she flipped open the lid and grabbed the closest donut within reach. She shoved a piece of it in her mouth and smiled in delight. She closed her eyes, savoring every sugary bite. Stevie cleared her throat, eagerly waiting for the information Zinny had promised.

"You gals better believe this'll be front page news." Zinny licked her fingers clean. "Mary Jean might kill me before my blood sugar does."

I wrinkled my nose.

What did Mary Jean have to do with anything?

"Don't be a drama queen, Zinny." Stevie rolled her eyes. "Just take the medication they give you, and you'll be fine."

"I'm sorry, did you say Mary Jean?" I tilted my head. "The same Mary Jean who still heckles us for our poor church attendance? The same Mary Jean who thinks Mardi Gras beads came from Satan's jewelry box?"

Zinny smirked and picked another donut. "That's the one."

"All right, you've had your fun." Stevie took the box of donuts and placed it across the room. "I don't want you dropping dead before you've told us what we need to know."

"Now I know where your priorities lie," she joked.

"What's going on with Mary Jean?" I asked, placing my hands on my hips. "What has she got to do with George Carmichael?" Zinny might have had a medical emergency, but every minute we lingered in her hospital room was a minute lost figuring out what really happened at the Crystal Grande Hotel.

"She paid me to keep quiet." Zinny lowered her voice and leaned closer to us. "She didn't want the public knowing her dirty deeds."

A shiver ran up my spine.

"Why are the strict conservative ones always the psychos?" Stevie shook her head.

Zinny chuckled as if the realization that Mary Jean wasn't as God-fearing as she seemed was the perfect present.

"Because they can't control themselves when they wander from the straight and narrow," Zinny muttered. She smirked and glanced at the door, making sure we wouldn't be interrupted. She cleared her throat. "George Carmichael was found dead in one of his own hotel rooms. What the papers aren't saying is that Room 111 wasn't vacant that night."

"You mean..." My eyes went wide. "The room was booked for the night?"

"Oh, yes." She raised her eyebrows.

"Booked by whom?" Stevie tapped her foot impatiently as the logic settled in. It wasn't long before her eyes were also wide with shock.

"Mary Jean, of course." Zinny chuckled again. "That dirty little harlot."

Chapter 11

He'd returned.

Our visit with Zinny had put everything back into perspective. Saving the bakery was all that mattered, and the weird vibe between me and Stevie could wait until after the police had cleared our little establishment of any foul play. We'd come home to a moving van next door. Our neighbor had returned from his latest trip to Chattanooga, where he'd sold his law practice in order to start over in Misty Key.

So far, he seemed like a nice guy, minus the fact that his parents hadn't been the most trustworthy of folks.

He was also a vampire.

"You've been busy, Mr. Larson." I watched as a team of movers carried a leather couch through the front door.

"Mr. Larson was my father," he responded. His fair skin and platinum hair looked even lighter in the afternoon sun. His tall and lanky stature reminded me of a blade of grass caught in an ocean breeze. I wasn't fooled by his fragile appearance. Vampires were a lot stronger than they looked, and Corpse Corp. owned a delivery service that supplied every registered vampire with a fair share of blood—all legally obtained. His twig-like arms could probably move mountains. "Call me Junior."

"I know you like to be called Junior," I admitted. "I'm just practicing that neighborly humor everyone around here is so fond of." Yogi sat next to my feet waiting to be taken on his afternoon walk. Stevie had gone back to the bakery, and I was glad. She stumbled over her words whenever Junior was around.

On second thought, I could've used the entertainment. It had been a long week.

"What about you?" he asked. "Are you the type to bring dinner to a starved man who has been moving all day?" Junior watched as another leather couch was carried into the house. "Barking orders is a lot more exhausting than you think."

"So, you're back in Misty Key for good?"

Whiskers walked cautiously through the front yard and stood next to Yogi. He looked up at me, and I suppressed an eye roll. I felt like a cat magnet, and I didn't know how to channel my magnetism toward something else. Like Aqua's bedroom. Or the gap behind my bookshelf.

"For now," Junior answered. "I sold all of my parents' old furniture. The whole medieval-antique style isn't really my thing."

"Bummer." I pushed back memories from the last time I'd been inside the house next door. I hoped Junior's décor wouldn't make me feel like I'd walked into a museum of precious artifacts. "I was really hoping to see one of those armored knights displayed on your doorstep. You know, a little something to spruce up your porch a bit."

"I bought a welcome mat." He shrugged.

"A welcome mat is a good start."

Yogi shook his collar and lay in the grass.

"Looks like he's given up." Junior glanced at Yogi with a grin. His pearly teeth were so perfect that I questioned whether or not they were real. And just like I didn't waltz around with a crystal ball offering to read people's palms, Junior didn't have fangs or an aversion to sunlight. The stereotypes placed on the magical world made me laugh sometimes.

"All right." I nudged Yogi with my foot. "Come on, boy. Let's get moving before the heat catches up to us." Even in February, there were afternoons where I'd found myself sweating under my blouse.

As I inched toward the sidewalk, Whiskers followed, and I wasn't surprised.

"So, that's a no to dinner then?" Junior crossed his arms, a charming smirk still on display.

"Oh, I'll be at the hotel tonight," I answered. "Haven't you heard?"

"I've been out of town, remember?" He shook his head, a symphony of banging going on behind him. One of the movers had knocked over a tower of boxes.

Yogi let out a short bark as if scolding the movers for their clumsiness.

"Tonight is the Mardi Gras kick-off party hosted by the Carmichael twins," I said.

"Right." Junior cleared his throat and paused for a minute to observe the chaos going on behind him. The movers quickly fixed their error. "I forgot about all that Mardi Gras stuff. I suppose the folks around here go all out?"

"Well, there's a parade tomorrow, and Stevie is selling out of king cakes as we speak."

Junior's expression changed when I said my sister's name. A subtle smile snuck across his face and then faded the moment he realized I'd noticed.

"Those cakes with the little babies inside?" he asked.

"Those are the ones," I responded. "And don't diss the babies. They're good luck."

"Sounds like a lawsuit waiting to happen." He chuckled. "All it would take is an ignorant customer who doesn't bother to chew before swallowing."

"I'll be sure to mention it to Stevie." This time I waited for the private smile, but Junior did the opposite when I said my sister's name again. In an attempt to hide his feelings, he clenched his jaw.

"Do or don't," he said. "It doesn't matter to me."
Nice save.

"You're new in town," I blurted out. "Why don't you join us tonight? You can tell Stevie all about our bakery's liabilities yourself."

"Oh, uh..."

"Sorry, you're probably busy." I took a deep breath. I'd been too hasty, but I knew Stevie would be less difficult to work with if Junior was around.

"No," he quickly replied. "No. I can adjust my schedule."

"Great. Then we'll see you tonight at the Crystal Grande Hotel."

* * *

"You are dead to me," Stevie whispered in my ear.

I was sure Whiskers had thought the same thing when I'd forced him to stay home with my mom.

I bit the corner of my lip, suppressing a smile. The four of us approached the entrance of the Crystal Grande Hotel, and Stevie stopped dead when she saw Junior lingering in the distance. The moon lit up the shoreline, and the outside of the hotel had been decorated with strings of gold, green, and purple lights. Music from inside floated through the night air and gave me butterflies. Thad walked next to me, and Aqua hadn't concealed the fact that she'd been studying our hands harder than all of her homework for the semester combined.

I wasn't going to grab Thad's hand, and I knew he wouldn't grab mine.

Especially not with Aqua glaring at the pair of us.

Along with music came the sound of chanting. It grew louder the closer we got to the entrance. The protestors were back blocking the front of the hotel, holding their signs and shouting their disapproval of the Carmichaels' celebration. I adjusted the top of my dress—a simple black number that Stevie had informed me was boring. But it hugged me in all the right places and paired with my wavy caramel hair, Thad didn't seem to mind. His eyes had lingered on me long enough my cheeks had started to feel hot. I'd blamed it on the humidity.

"Not these crazies again," Aqua muttered, eyeing the group in front of the main entrance. "The front of the hotel is like a prime selfie spot, and those guys are ruining it."

"There are more important things than selfies," Stevie muttered through her teeth. As Junior smiled and walked toward us, she nervously adjusted her dress too.

"Admit it, Stevie." I lowered my voice so only she could hear me. "You wish you were wearing something *boring* right about now. Well, forget it. I'm not switching dresses with you. My boobs would pop right out of that thing."

"Oh, shut up," she murmured back, standing up straighter in an attempt to prove me wrong. Stevie had thrown on the flashiest thing in her closet, which had turned out to be something short and strapless with green sequins. She'd claimed it was Mardi Gras appropriate and that showing off her sleeve of tattoos wasn't something she had the opportunity to do very often.

"Why is she scratching? And why is she standing like that?" Aqua narrowed her eyes and observed Stevie scratch the side of her arm. She hunched her shoulders, covering the front of her dress as she said hello to Junior.

"Vampires tend to have that effect on people," Thad muttered. "Oh, she also has a thing for him."

"You can tell all that just by an itch?" Aqua batted her long eyelashes, proud of her attire. She wore a flowy blue dress that embodied her name. It reminded me of a waterfall—a perky, cute waterfall. "Interesting."

"I can sense it." He pointed to his nose. "Animal instincts, remember?"

"I'd better watch out then." Aqua snuck a playful glance in my direction and pushed her way through a wall of protestors. She disappeared inside the hotel, leaving me alone with Thad.

I wondered what he'd sensed about me. My chest went tight just thinking about it. Suddenly, I had a hard time looking him in the eyes. What if he read into the things I did and said? If this was what it felt like to hang out with a psychic, then I was getting a taste of my own medicine, and it didn't taste good at all.

My gaze caught sight of something strong enough to douse my insecurities.

It was Mary Jean. She was front and center and shouting the loudest of them all.

My cheeks burned with disappointment.

Disappointment that she had the nerve to preach to others the things she hadn't mastered herself. I crossed my arms and watched her heckle a young valet returning from parking a guest's car. Mary Jean even had the nerve to chastise the hired help, although all of them were just there for the paycheck.

"What's wrong?" Thad studied me. A light ocean breeze pushed the scent of his cologne straight toward me. The earthy smell laced with a bit of peppermint was enough to make me lose my focus. "Did you see something? Is it numbers?"

"Mary Jean." I cleared my throat and reminded myself of my objective—to help Stevie contact the ghost of George Carmichael and seize any other sleuthing opportunities that came my way.

"I'm not much of church-goer so..."

"Excuse me while I address the dirt under the rug." I strutted toward Mary Jean, and it took her a moment to stop glaring at me and realize who I was. The sound of chanting dropped considerably as she stepped aside, lowering her sign.

"Oh, not you too," Mary Jean stated, giving my outfit a once-over. She shrugged. I knew my dress was more modest than most.

But Mary Jean's eyes grew to the size of chocolate cupcakes when Stevie stood at my side.

"Step back before you give her a heart attack," I muttered.

"Go ahead, Mary Jean," Stevie responded, spinning around so that Mary Jean saw her sequined dress from all angles. "Drink it in."

"You should be ashamed of yourself, leaving the house looking like a..."

"Slut?" Stevie happily finished. "Hooker? Common prostitute? Or my favorite, *home-wrecker*?"

"Oh, no." I rubbed the side of my forehead. Stevie's approach at questioning someone was much different than mine. For one, she liked to push buttons. And more than anything, she liked to start arguments she knew she could win.

"*Yes* to all of the above." Mary Jean nodded, smoothing her plain white T-shirt and loose cardigan that made her torso look like a shapeless blob.

"Unbelievable. You're such a hypocrite." Stevie gave her one of her classic stares.

"Excuse me?" Mary Jean scowled in response.

"Enough," I said to Stevie, stepping in between her and Mary Jean.

"Mary Jean, you've been a customer of ours for a very long time—"

"Not much longer if your sister continues dressing like that," Mary Jean interrupted, pointing at Stevie.

"My point is that our family bakery has served the folks in this town since I was a little girl, and it would be a shame to let all of that go down the drain."

"I don't understand what you're getting at." Mary Jean tilted her head, a smug expression on her face. "I have the right to voice my opinions just like everybody else. But, of course, since my opinions don't align with the majority, people think I'm insane."

"That's not what I'm talking about." I took a deep breath. Approaching things in life from a logical standpoint worked some of the time. This wasn't one of those times.

"We know about you and George Carmichael," Stevie blurted out.

Mary Jean's face went as white as a sheet.

Her condescending glare was wiped clean as she stared straight ahead of her, ignoring both Stevie and me. A couple of short breaths escaped her mouth, and her chest heaved as if she'd just finished a mile-long sprint. I extended a hand toward her but she slapped it away.

"What do you know exactly?" she breathed.

"The hotel room where he was found was booked under your name," Stevie said. "Do you care to explain that?"

"I..." Her breathing became increasingly unsteady.

"Were you two having an affair?" Stevie raised her eyebrows.

"No," Mary Jean barked. The color returned to her face. "No! It wasn't like that at all, and I suggest you get your facts straight before you start spreading rumors. Bad things happen to gossipers. Don't you two know that?"

"Mary Jean, why did you book that hotel room?" I asked. "I'm not accusing you of adultery. We're just trying to figure out what happened because—"

"Take the lobby!" A fire lit in Mary Jean's eyes as she raised her sign as high as she could and screamed at her posse to charge the front entrance.

Mary Jean turned away from us and led her group of protestors into the lobby of the hotel. A wave of valets hurried to push them back out, but they were useless. The shouting and chanting echoed once they'd made their way inside, and a look of horror crossed the face of the woman sitting at the reception desk.

Stevie placed a hand on her hips. "Well, that took a turn for the worst."

"You did egg her on talking about sluts and home-wreckers," I commented.

A large gap of space waited between us and the crowded front entrance. It had been difficult before to push through the crowd of protestors and make it inside. Now that Mary Jean and her gang occupied the lobby, it would be impossible to make it to the party. We would have to use another entrance.

"Quite the welcoming committee." Junior joined us along with Thad.

The four of us observed the pandemonium as another calming ocean breeze blew across our faces.

"The start of an interesting night," Thad added.

"I'm sure the worst is yet to come," Stevie teased. "I swear the Crystal Grande is cursed."

"If your psychic senses say so," Junior replied.

"My psychic senses are telling me that the cops will be here any second," I added.

"More numbers?" Thad eagerly searched our surroundings.

I pointed at the flashing lights speeding their way up the hill. "Sure. I'm *that* good."

Chapter 12

Something grabbed my arm, and I jumped.

"Fancy meeting you here." Rickiah Pepper wore a lively red cocktail dress. Her smile glowed as did her bronze skin. She didn't seem as concerned as some of the other guests about the various police officers patrolling the main level of the hotel.

"Geez, Rickiah," I breathed.

"Why so tense?" She raised her eyebrows, but then nodded when she spotted Thad. "Never mind. I can draw my own conclusions, thank you. And where exactly is the rest of your crew?"

"Aqua will be somewhere on the dance floor," I responded. "And, uh...Stevie is over there *looking for evidence*." I tilted my head in Stevie's direction. She stood twirling a strand of her midnight locks as she listened to Junior explain the meaning of the word *comestible*. She was standing less than a foot away from a platter of beignets, and she hadn't even bothered to taste and critique them.

"So, the neighbor is back, is he?" Rickiah pursed her lips.

I nodded and clapped when the jazz band at the head of the ballroom concluded their number and bowed, making room for another group to go on stage and keep the festive tempo flowing. The entire room had been decorated with enough lights and banners to make anyone feel like they were inches away from Bourbon Street.

An employee circled the room for the tenth time passing out beads and hats. I was running out of room around my neck, and I was pretty sure my chest lit up every time a spotlight was pointed in my direction. A New Orleans–style buffet took up an entire wall with enough king cakes for all of Misty Key.

Jewel Carmichael was near the stage chatting with several of her admirers, a security guard preventing anyone from touching her or taking pictures without her permission. Her twin brother, Jonathon, sat in a corner of the ballroom that had been fashioned into a VIP lounge. Women in dresses even more revealing than Stevie's giggled on both sides of him.

"They seem like they're taking their father's death rather hard." Rickiah eyed Jewel as she batted her eyelashes and pretended not to notice the catcalls and whistling as she stepped on stage to thank everyone for coming.

"You never know what goes on behind closed doors," I commented.

Thad took a step closer to me, and I instinctively took a step away. Part of me was paranoid he could somehow sense my thoughts. Not that my thoughts were that revealing. They mostly consisted of the Carmichael case and the trouble the bakery was in.

"Speaking of which, I don't see the missus," Thad added.

"Mrs. Carmichael?" I searched the crowd.

"Rumor on the street is she hasn't left her room since her husband died. Again." Rickiah shrugged. "So sad."

"Those rumors are true," Thad confirmed. "No one has seen her all week. I mean, apart from the police."

I gulped, remembering the moment I'd stumbled into Room 111 and had seen for myself the sad fate of George Carmichael. How unlucky to have been lost at sea only to be rescued and then murdered. I swallowed hard, knowing there was more to the story than what the papers had reported.

"I've seen enough," I said, crossing my arms and glancing at Stevie. "I think it's time we do what we came here to do."

"Which is?" Rickiah placed her hands on her hips. "Oh no. Please tell me you didn't come here just to go snooping around where you don't belong." Her eyes darted to the buffet table. "I haven't even had a slice of king cake yet."

"Then go and grab one," I replied. "And pray you get the slice with the baby in it because we're going to need all the luck we can get."

As if sensing my frustration, Stevie and Junior returned to the group nibbling on petit fours that had been dusted with edible gold glitter. Stevie held up the sweet and studied each layer before wrinkling her nose.

"I can make a moister cake than this," she muttered, crumbling the dessert up in her napkin.

"Shall we?" My eyes darted to the exit.

My heart pounded as I led the way back toward the lobby. A group of police officers stood at the front entrance, preventing protestors from rushing into the hotel again. Mary Jean's voice echoed in the back of my mind as my eyes fixated on the hallway leading to Room 111. I was surprised Mary Jean was still outside chanting after our confrontation. I knew it was only a matter of time before her true relationship with George Carmichael came out. Zinny would see to that once she returned to work at the *Misty Messenger*.

Memories of flashing numbers circled my brain as we neared the crime scene. Suddenly, my throat felt dry, and I wanted nothing more than to turn around and let Stevie do her thing alone. But I couldn't. I had to face my fears and enter Room 111 again for the bakery's sake. I glanced over my shoulder and gulped when I noticed that everyone, minus my little sister, Aqua, had tagged along for the ride. Thad was close behind me with clenched fists. Junior stayed next to Stevie, and Rickiah studied each room number like she expected to find a clue from the killer taped to a door.

"How are the numbers looking?" Thad whispered. He leaned in so close I caught a whiff of his minty breath.

"Quiet." But the truth was that the same numbers that had been screaming at me the day of Mr. Carmichael's death were still shouting just as loudly.

That meant one of two things.

The ghost of George Carmichael was still around.

Or another body was waiting to be discovered.

My entire torso froze. We'd arrived at our destination too quickly, and standing in front of the room that had changed everything for me and the family bakery made a wave of nausea wash over my stomach. I stood and stared. I didn't know whether to knock or to just walk right in. The thought that anything could be waiting for me on the other side of the door sent chills down my spine.

"Hello, Ember?" The sound of Stevie's voice brought me back to the present. "Are you even listening to me?"

I turned around, wiping a subtle bead of sweat from my forehead.

"What?"

"How are we going to get in?" Stevie impatiently stepped past me and tried the doorknob. "See? It's locked. Not a surprise."

"There's a master key in the manager's office," Thad said.

"If you need to charm someone, I'm your man," Junior said, his expression bleeding with confidence.

Thad wrinkled his forehead, studying the look on Junior's face for the first time since meeting him.

"You?" Thad chuckled to himself.

"Don't underestimate vampire charm, wolf boy." Junior smirked, hardly paying attention to Thad as he took a step toward him. They matched each other in height, but Thad clearly outweighed Junior when it came to muscle. But it was still unclear what sort of strength Junior really possessed. None of us had seen him in action.

"*Wolf boy?*" Thad repeated. "I'm sorry, who invited you along? This is a private matter. Friends only."

"Neighbors *are* friends," he replied. "And where exactly do you live?"

A fiery glimmer flashed in Thad's eyes. Junior knew exactly how to tease the wild animal in him. The question was could Thad resist? Stevie and I exchanged nervous glances as Rickiah sized up each one of them like she was deciding which one would win in a fist fight.

"OK, this isn't a nineties soap opera," Stevie interrupted. "You two obviously can't be left alone together. *I'll* go with Junior to the manager's office. Rickiah, you come and help me keep watch in case we have to break in. Thad, you stay here with Ember."

"Excellent plan, Stevie." Rickiah smiled widely and winked at me.

The three of them wasted no time jogging down the hall toward the kitchen and employee lounge. I didn't doubt that they would figure out a solution to our problem. I did doubt my ability to step back into the crime scene once they returned. I hadn't let myself dwell on the day I found George Carmichael's body, and the memories began flooding my mind until I felt like I was drowning.

What if Stevie couldn't connect with Mr. Carmichael?

What if the bakery made national news for killing a famous billionaire?

What if the family business tanked big time?

What if I took that job in New York City?

"Ember?" Thad observed every curve of my face. "Are you sure you're OK?"

"Yeah," I lied, forcing myself to remain expressionless. But the more time I spent in Misty Key, the more my defenses weakened. I'd noticed a couple of weeks ago when one of Stevie's reality TV shows had brought a tear to my eye. The icy demeanor I'd been known for at Fillmore Media was quickly melting away. And Thad saw right through me.

"You know I know you're lying." Thad gently pointed to his nose. His sharp features contrasted with his soft countenance, which he seemed to reserve just for me.

"I'm getting worse and worse at lying every day." I shrugged and forced myself to smile. "Small-town syndrome?"

"Isn't it the pits?" Thad rolled up the sleeves of his navy button-down and crossed his arms. "I knew returning Miss Betty's lost puppy would be the end of me. Now it's all icebox cakes, pralines, and free sweet tea around here. My days of being the mysterious outsider are numbered."

I let out a giggle. "I know, it's horrible."

"Why can't we go back to being our usual uncaring selves?" Thad shook his head, grinning when he noticed that his words made me smile even more.

"Well, I might get the chance," I blurted out, unsure why I'd said it.

"What do you mean?"

"Uh…" I cleared my throat. "I guess maybe I should tell someone. My old boss called and offered me a job."

"The guy who gave your promotion to someone else?"

"That's the one," I answered. "Except he offered me that director position and a raise."

Thad exhaled loudly and nodded. If he were Stevie, he would tell me I was selfish for even considering it. If he were my mother, he'd tell me to follow my heart. I could predict my family's opinions word for word, and those opinions had already floated in one ear and out the other.

Thad was different. I couldn't predict what he'd say to me. He wasn't family, and yet I found myself fearing his reaction the most. Would my decision change his opinion of me? I hated that I cared so much.

"What did you say?" Thad asked.

"I told him I would sleep on it." I touched my cheek and thought back to the moment I'd taken the phone call. "I mean, my first instinct was to say no."

"But then you got thinking," Thad finished.

"Yeah." I clasped my hands in front of me and scanned the hallway. "I thought I knew what I wanted, but I guess I don't. Otherwise, saying no would have been easy, right?" I looked to him for reassurance.

"Not necessarily." He leaned closer so that the side of his arm grazed against mine. "Sometimes we make life-changing decisions and then life throws us curveballs."

"I wish I knew why."

"It's a test," Thad explained. "To see how bad you want something. I guess you need to choose what you want and sink your whole heart into it."

"And if I choose New York again?" I looked at him, and our eyes connected. I couldn't help but get lost in the shades of hickory surrounding his pupils.

"If that's what will make you happy."

"You obviously don't have sisters," I said. "They might never speak to me again."

"I'm sure they would understand in time." Thad took a step closer. "Are you seriously considering leaving?"

I took a deep breath.

Something flashed in the corner of my eye.

It was a number down the hall, and it was new.

I narrowed my eyes and took a step toward it.

"What is it?" Thad followed my gaze. "What do you see?"

"Unhappy numbers." The number nine glowed, growing brighter and brighter until I took a few steps closer. Another number flickered even further down the hall. Another nine. Then an eleven. Then seventeen. My pulse quickened. The numbers wanted me to venture deeper into the hotel.

The numbers wanted to show me something.

Thad stayed by my side as I turned a corner, walked down another hallway of guest rooms, and then turned again. I'd been to the Crystal Grande several times, and I knew where everything was. The numbers were leading me to...

"The beach?" Thad whispered.

We'd reached an exit for guests only that led to the private stretch of beach owned by the Carmichaels. Looking through the glass door, I didn't see much. The sky was dark, and the moon was hidden behind thick clouds. I slowly pushed open the door and immediately felt a brisk sea breeze rush across my cheeks.

"The beach it is," I muttered, taking a step into the evening humidity.

"Wait." Thad grabbed my hand, sending a ray of warmth through my torso. "The others will be back with a key soon. We should wait for them."

"Whatever I'm meant to see might be gone." My heart drummed. I told myself it was psychic nerves and the thrill that came with using my gift successfully.

Thad took a moment to sniff the air before gesturing toward the sugar sand. I stepped outside, my eyes darting to every corner of my surroundings. I waved at Thad to follow me.

"Hold on. Try the handle first." Thad nudged me out of the way and then shut the door completely. From the outside, I tried to open it again. It was locked, and I saw where the guest key card needed to be inserted. I knocked gently and Thad opened it. "See? You won't be able to get back in. I'll have to wait for you here."

"How inconvenient." Another breeze blew through my hair.

"Go ahead," Thad said. "Check it out, and I'll be right here when you get back."

"And if I get into trouble?" I bit the corner of my lip.

"Scream."

Thad softly closed the door, leaving me alone with the tide. The sound of waves crashing against the shore grew louder as my feet hit the sand. I took off my shoes, letting the serenity of my surroundings engulf every part of me. I desperately needed the calm in my life, and the Gulf had always provided that. It was a feeling I couldn't get in the big city.

My gaze moved up and down the shore.

A few couples from the party stumbled across the sand holding drinks and flashlights.

And past the hotel, a woman stood near the water.

I squinted, studying her elegant cocktail dress and sparkly gold scarf that fluttered in the wind.

It was Mrs. Carmichael.

"Seriously?" I muttered, looking back at the hotel. "*That's* what you wanted to show me?" The numbers spoke to me, but I couldn't say anything back. Although sometimes it was worth a try.

My toes curled in the sand with every step I took. I had no idea what to say to Mrs. Carmichael. I'd had brief encounters with her in the past, but none long enough for her to remember my name or anything about me.

Mrs. Carmichael spotted me and automatically straightened her shoulders. Her hand dabbed at a spot underneath her eye. From what I could see, it looked like she'd been crying. I slowed my pace and moved closer to the sea. A tiny wave reached my toes. The water was cool but not ice cold.

"Beautiful night." I looked up at the sky, unable to see many stars.

"If you like storm clouds," Mrs. Carmichael replied. She was even more petite up close. Her hair was shades lighter than her son's. It almost matched the golden tone of her scarf. A shiny acrylic nail scratched the side of her head. "A woman from Cottonberry does it."

"Does what?"

"My hair." Mrs. Carmichael looked me up and down. "If you're going to stare, you might as well ask."

"Oh..." I twiddled my fingers. "Sorry, I didn't realize I was staring."

"So, you're not from the papers?" Her lips twisted into a pseudo-smile.

"Why, do you have gray hairs you don't want anyone to know about?" I paused. It probably wasn't the best comment to make, but I figured she'd gotten enough sorries and condolences from just about everyone in her life.

"Quite a few." Her smile became a bit more genuine. "Sorry, honey. When you're a Carmichael, everyone around you has a hidden agenda."

"Understandable," I agreed.

"What's yours?"

The question pierced the night like an arrow sailing toward a bullseye.

"To say thank you," I responded, thinking quick on my feet.

"Oh." She raised her eyebrows. "And what are you thanking me for?"

"For...putting a stop to the remodel," I stammered. "Yes. The remodel. The Crystal Grande is such a beautiful place. I've been coming here since I was a kid. It would have been a shame to see the place gutted."

"Stopping the remodel was my husband's doing," she said. "He came in and fired people. He even terminated the contract I'd made with my new business partner, Indie Wilkes. He didn't like Indie at all."

"Right." I took a deep breath.

"What's your name?" Mrs. Carmichael narrowed her eyes and glanced at my dress.

"Ember."

"Your last name?"

"Greene," I added.

Her gaze fell to my hands.

"No husband?" she asked.

"Nope." I held up my hands and showed off my naked fingers.

"Boyfriend?"

"No." I shook my head.

"Wait a minute. *Greene.* Your family owns Lunar Bakery. That's it."

"Yes," I said.

"Your parents are lucky to have such devoted children." She tilted her head toward the hotel. "I wish the twins were interested in the family business. All they seem to care about is reaping the rewards. I suppose that's partly my fault. I just wanted them to have everything I didn't."

"Give it a few years," I responded. "Things could change."

"There are too many temptations in this world for children like Jewel and Jonathon. At least I've managed to keep them here in Misty Key where I can keep an eye on them. It's been hard with their father gone." She touched a spot beneath her eye and sniffled.

"My mom lights candles."

"Excuse me?"

"She lights candles," I explained. "It helps her deal with the stress. Every night, the house is full of them. Lavender and vanilla. You should try it."

"Thanks, dear, but my situation probably calls for something a little stronger."

"Yep. She's got bottles of that too." I raised my eyebrows. "It was really hard on her when my dad first passed, but she gets better every year."

Mrs. Carmichael rested a hand underneath her chin. Her eyes passed over me with a look of concern, as if she'd changed her opinion of me in a matter of minutes. She narrowed her eyes.

"And what about you, Ember?"

"The hole in my heart will always be there," I confessed. "Time doesn't heal wounds. It just makes room for scars." It was true. No matter how much time had gone by, it still felt like yesterday that my father passed on to the other side. The hardest part was that he hadn't come back to communicate with Stevie at all. He must have thought it was easier that way.

"Yes, but can you live with scars?" Mrs. Carmichael asked.

"Ask me again in a few years, ma'am."

"Call me Elizabeth," she responded. "Tell me, Ember, what's a bright woman like you doing working at a bakery?"

"Oh, I didn't always work at the bakery. I used to work in the Big Apple, believe it or not."

"That explains the accent." She grinned. "Or lack thereof."

"I get that a lot." I shrugged. "What can I say? I'm just being me."

"You know the police think my husband was murdered." Mrs. Carmichael took in the subtle breeze and gazed up and down the beach. "I'm sure you've read the papers."

"Is that what you think too?"

"Yes." She nodded. "My husband had lots of enemies." Her eyes fixated on a figure that approached us. She waved. "The remodel. Selling half of the hotel. I hope you can understand that I *don't* wish to follow in my husband's footsteps."

"There you are." The figure morphed into a man, who stopped beside Mrs. Carmichael and kissed her firmly on the cheek. He extended a hand to me. "Hello, there. And you are?"

"Ember Greene." I shook his hand because he didn't give me the option not to. The two of us were at the same eye level. He was almost as petite as Mrs. Carmichael, but he carried himself with suave and charisma.

"This is Harrison," Mrs. Carmichael said. "He's my latest business partner."

"You found another investor?"

"I sure did," she answered. "Harrison and I have entered into a new contract as equal partners. In all honesty, I can't keep this place running all by myself."

"That's where I come in." Harrison grinned and held out his arm. Mrs. Carmichael wrapped her hand around his small bicep. "And you can call me Mr. H. Everyone else at the hotel does. Shall we, my dear?"

"I suppose I should make some sort of appearance at my own party." Mrs. Carmichael straightened her scarf and smoothed her golden hair.

"Brave face, hon." Harrison patted her hand. "This will all blow over in a month, and then we can move forward with our plans."

"Plans?" I repeated.

Mr. H raised his eyebrows, revealing deep creases on his forehead.

"I'm moving forward with the remodel." Mrs. Carmichael nodded as if her mind had been made up. "But maybe I can make a few tweaks to the design. You and I should have coffee."

"Sure."

"I'll be in touch," Mrs. Carmichael replied.

I wasn't sure if she was the sort who tossed around empty words or if she meant what she said.

I guessed I would soon find out.

Chapter 13

Stevie stared daggers in my direction.

"Nice of you to show up." Stevie stamped her foot as she leaned against the wall across from Room 111. "I was just about to call Detective Winter."

"No you weren't," Thad answered for me. As promised, he'd waited patiently for me to return from my beach adventure so he could let me back into the hotel.

"Where did the two of you run off to?" Rickiah looked at me and then at Thad. When her gaze fell to his lips, I knew what she was thinking. A sly smile crossed her face. I was too distracted with the conversation I'd just had with Mrs. Carmichael to blush.

"I saw numbers," I replied to the group. "I had to leave. I'm sorry."

"And?" Stevie shrugged. "Have you solved the case? Can we all go home?"

"Speak for yourself," Rickiah muttered. "Mardi Gras is in full swing in the ballroom, and I'm not leaving until I get a dadgum slice of king cake."

"I swear food is all you talk about sometimes." Stevie directed her negative vibes away from me for once. Apparently, Junior's charm had worn off, because she was back to her usual pissed-off self.

"Did you get a key?" I interrupted. Rickiah wasn't like me. She didn't pass up opportunities to argue, and she would have bickered with Stevie all night.

"It was the charm." Junior stepped forward with a grin. He handed me a room key, his eyes briefly darting in Thad's direction.

"Yeah." Rickiah laughed. "He *charmed* that lock on the door right open."

Junior cleared his throat and ignored Rickiah's comment.

I tried the key, and my stomach churned when it worked. The door to Room 111 creaked open, revealing darkness on the other side. I hesitated, but Stevie walked right past me and flipped on a light. I gulped.

The room had been cleaned. The bed was made but the memory of George's body haunted the back of my brain. I glanced at the table where I'd seen a slice of red velvet cheesecake and a cake box with the bakery's logo. The table was clear, and the smell of cleaning chemicals still lingered in the air. I rubbed my arms, getting goose bumps. The room was colder than the hallway.

Stevie followed her usual routine when trying to contact the dead. She quietly walked along the perimeter of the room, lightly dragging her fingers on the wall and pausing every so often as if someone was speaking to her. Junior watched her work with great interest while Rickiah observed the room with a disappointed expression. Thad's shoulder brushed against mine. I'd hardly moved at all.

"You would think they'd splurge for a higher thread count." Rickiah pursed her lips, rubbing a section of bed sheets in between her fingers. "And the towels in the bathroom aren't very soft. I can't believe people spend hundreds of dollars a night for *this*."

Stevie cleared her throat, and Rickiah quickly shut her mouth.

Stevie took a deep breath and stopped at a tall mahogany dresser.

"Strange." Stevie tilted her head, adjusting the bust line of her dress as she touched the shiny wooden surface. "Mr. Carmichael is definitely still around, but..." She left the dresser and proceeded to a closet next to the bed. She moved aside the sliding door and frowned when she was met with empty hangers and not much else.

"What is it?" My voice was low and a little shaky. I placed a hand on my chest and forced myself to take long, calming breaths.

"I hear him, but..." Stevie looked around the room again before her eyes fixated on me. "Are you sure he died in *this* room?"

I nodded. "I'm positive."

"Well, is there another room on the other side of this wall?" She closed the closet and pressed her hand against the neighboring wallpaper.

"No," Rickiah answered. "This is a corner room. There's nothing but beach on the other side of that wall."

Stevie quietly cursed to herself and rolled her eyes. She looked up at the ceiling.

"What kind of game are you playing here, George?" Stevie shouted. "Come talk to me or leave. It's as simple as that." She muttered a few curse words. "Geez, some spirits have absolutely no manners."

Thad walked toward the closet, sniffing the atmosphere.

"Excuse me." Thad slid open the closet door and looked inside.

"It's like he's in the walls or something," Stevie commented. "Whatever he's getting at, I don't get it."

Thad knocked on the wall inside the closet and stopped when he came to a spot that didn't sound like the others. He knocked again and pressed his ear to the wall. Grinning, he took a step back and then kicked the wall in the closet with all of his might.

Crash.

My heart jumped.

"Hey, buddy," Rickiah called out from across the room. She'd taken a few steps back until she'd reached the bathroom. "I'm pretty sure that's considered vandalism."

"She's right," Junior agreed. "The hotel could sue."

"Only if one of you rats me out," Thad pointed out. He kicked the wall again and a slight yelped escaped Rickiah's lips.

"How about a warning next time," Rickiah scolded him.

But I paid little attention.

I was too busy focusing on the gaping hole in front of me. A piece of the wall had caved in and the hole was a perfect rectangle. Thad had kicked in a secret door in the closet. He stood back, admired his handiwork, and gestured at the darkened hallway on the other side. A slight smirk crossed Thad's face. He seemed to be enjoying Stevie's shocked expression. He'd rendered her speechless.

"I present to you a secret passageway," Thad announced.

"Of course," Junior chimed in. "A classic addition to any historical structure. I was just about to suggest that."

"I'm sure you were," Thad murmured.

Stevie led the way, using the light from her cell phone to push away the shadows on either side of her. She flashed her phone in one direction and chuckled as she entered the secret hallway and opened a miniature door. An ocean breeze rushed inside.

"Will you look at that," Stevie commented. "This door leads to the beach." She shut it and walked in the other direction where she was met with a narrow staircase. "And I bet this leads to some secret entrance on every floor."

"Or perhaps it goes all the way up to the Carmichael suites?" I suggested.

"Is this what you wanted me to find, George?" Stevie shouted up the stairs. "You're a very clever man. There, I said it. Will you please come and talk to me now?"

Stevie paused as if listening to a faint reply. She tilted her head toward the staircase and waved at the rest of us to follow her. One-by-one, we entered the tight passageway in the closet of Room 111. Junior followed Stevie. Rickiah followed Junior, and Thad insisted that he go last. He shut the closet door behind us, concealing our presence at the crime scene completely.

The glow from all of our cell phones lit the way. The staircase was so narrow that walls touched both of my shoulders. I looked behind me and saw Thad walking up the stairs sideways. A musty smell filled my nostrils as I climbed step after step. As I'd predicted, the passage led all the way to the Carmichael suites on the top floor.

Stevie stopped in front of another rectangular crack in the wall. She gently pushed it, hesitating to use as much force as Thad had. The hallway was much too narrow for Thad to move all the way up front without stepping on all of us first.

"I can't open it." Stevie's voice floated toward me like a ghostly whisper.

"Muscle it open," Thad responded. "We can fix it later."

"Yeah," Rickiah added. "Some of us start to lose our minds when we're in confined spaces for too long." The sound of her heavy breathing filled my ears.

"Close your eyes," I suggested.

"Girl, that makes it worse," she muttered. "Oh, I think I'm gonna be sick."

"All right, chill out," Stevie said. "I'll try again."

A bang echoed through the confined hall and pierced my ear drums like the sound of gunshot. My heart raced, unable to stop as ray of light illuminated the path in front of me. One-by-one, each of us exited the secret passageway and stepped into another spacious closet.

"Holy *Chanel*," Rickiah muttered. Her eyes went wide as she reached for a dress hanging in front of her face. "This dress costs more than my car."

The rest of us stepped into a large bedroom with a king-sized bed, a sitting area the size of my mother's living room, and giant windows draped with ivory curtains. Rickiah gasped as she walked into the adjoining bathroom and began muttering the names of countless designers, some of which I hadn't even heard of before I'd moved to New York.

"This must be Mrs. Carmichael's room," I said, my eyes darting to a chandelier that graced the sitting area. "Lucky for us she's at the party right now with her new business partner."

"OK, I'm impressed, George." Stevie paced the room. "You're a genius. Is that what you wanted me to say?" She paused and then exhaled loudly. "Finally. He's here."

I clenched my jaw. Stevie was alarmingly comfortable with the dead, which was understandable, given her talent. But I wasn't. And from the looks of it, neither were Rickiah or Thad.

"Did he say who killed him?" I asked, hoping for a quick and easy answer to the riddle.

"He's explaining to me how he designed this whole floor." Stevie shook her head. "Yes, we know you designed you family's suites yourself. The whole town knows that." She placed her hands on her hips.

"What's he saying now?" Rickiah chimed in.

"How brilliant he is for putting secret passageways in his hotel so his family can come and go as they please without being photographed," Stevie answered. She stared at the empty space in front of her and tapped her foot. "Yes, but who killed you?" She rolled her eyes like she was talking with a family member. "What? Now you're quiet all of a sudden?"

"What kind of man doesn't want to avenge his own death?" Rickiah moved to the nightstand and continued her snooping.

"OK." Stevie took a deep breath. "OK. George says he doesn't know."

"What do you mean he doesn't know?" Thad crossed his arms. "Who was with him when he died?"

"Well, you heard him," Stevie said. "Who was with you in Room 111?" She paused for a moment and then scowled. "What do you mean no one? You expect me to believe you weren't waiting for someone? Like a special lady friend perhaps?"

My heart pounded. Stevie was thinking of Mary Jean, but I couldn't fathom the idea of George and Mary Jean being intimate. No. There had to be something else. I tried to calm my nerves, but it was no use. My hands shook as I approached Stevie.

I had to grab her hand.

Stevie's gift had evolved over the past year, as some gifts did, and she had the ability to transfer what she saw to a blood relative with a simple touch. The last time I'd taken Stevie's hand during one of her ghostly encounters had haunted me for weeks.

But I grabbed her hand anyway.

Stevie looked down at our interlocked fingers with a look of surprise.

Immediately, a figure formed in front of me. Soft whispers lingered in my ears, and I saw the face of the late George Carmichael. He looked like he had before he died, and when he spoke, it sounded like I was listening from far away. I concentrated as hard as I could.

"I told you," George said. I squinted, observing the creases under his eyes. "I walked into the room. I had my coffee. I changed into my robe and sat on the bed, and then poof. Lights out."

I didn't remember a coffee cup, but I could have missed it.

"So, there was no red velvet cheesecake?" I asked.

My entire body froze as George turned and looked right at me.

He threw his hands in the air.

"Great. Now *she* can see me too? Why don't we just call a press conference while we're at it?"

"She can see you because she's my sister," Stevie explained, holding up our hands. "She can see you because I'm letting her see you. Now, Ember asked you a question, and we've gone along with your little games, Mr. Carmichael. Did you see a cheesecake?"

"No," George answered, his fuzzy frame jumping to the other end of the room.

"You're only hurting your family here," Stevie pointed out. "Don't they deserve to know what happened to you? Unless you're hiding something?"

"I'm dead, my friend." George's figure moved again. This time it was up toward the ceiling. "I have no secrets anymore."

Mary Jean's face flashed in my head. I remembered the pale shade of her cheeks when Stevie had insinuated that she was a home-wrecker. George had to be lying. And even in death, he was still lying. Why? Who was he trying to protect? Surely he wasn't hiding the identity of his attacker. Why would he do that?

"Then admit you had a mistress," I blurted out. I could have been right, and I could have been wrong, but saying it out loud would confirm my suspicions.

Sure enough, George went as pale as a ghost can go.

"Ah-ha!" Stevie pointed her finger at the ceiling. "So you are hiding something."

"That's preposterous," George argued, his spirit jumping back to where it had first appeared.

"Then tell us who she is," Stevie insisted.

"Fine. I had a mistress. But I'm not saying her name. She's still alive, and I have to protect her privacy." George nodded with the same condescending glare I'd seen used by every member of the Carmichael family.

"I'm not the paparazzi, George." Stevie pulled at the hem of her dress, trying to yank it down so it covered more of her thigh. She was unsuccessful. "I'm not going to slather her name all over the news. I'm not going to spray paint it all over Main Street."

"I can't tell you."

"Even if she murdered you?" I added.

"She would never!" George shouted, his shadowy figure bouncing straight toward my face. I stumbled back, keeping hold of my sister's hand.

"How do you know that?" Stevie cleared her throat, attempting to steer his attention in another direction. "You said you didn't see anyone."

"Yes, but..." George's ghost darted toward Stevie this time, and she didn't seem the least bit frightened. I still didn't know how she coped with the things she saw.

"We're very discreet," Stevie assured him. "Was it Mary Jean?"

George frowned.

"Who?"

"Mary Jean Covey," Stevie answered. "The hotel room was booked in her name the day you died."

"Anyone could have paid her to book that room." The words flew out of George's mouth like a stream of fresh water.

"So, you're saying your mistress paid Mary Jean to book that room for your little rendezvous?" Stevie glared at him.

"No...I don't know...oh, you're confusing me." George's ghost got fuzzier and fuzzier. At first, I thought I'd loosened my grip on Stevie's hand.

"Hey!" Stevie shouted. George's spirit came back into view. "We're not finished here."

"I think we are," George replied.

"I don't understand you." Stevie raised her voice even louder. "I'm giving you the chance to come clean. To name your killer. To give your family some peace of mind and—"

"You think my family cares about what happened to me?" George's ghost was suddenly clear. The clearest I'd seen any spirit. He looked like he'd stepped straight out of his portrait in the lobby, and his suit was neatly pressed like he'd been planning on attending the festivities downstairs. He looked as if nothing had changed.

"Of course they care." A concerned expression lingered on Stevie's face. "They're family. And they lost you twice, George. Not once. *Twice.*"

"They didn't lose me twice," George smugly replied. "Because I was never lost in the first place."

Stevie narrowed her eyes.

"You mean to say you've been here in Misty Key all these years?"

"That is correct," George admitted. "You see, with my passageways I came and went as I pleased."

"And you faked your death why?" Stevie's eyes went wide.

"Some very dangerous people were after me, and it seemed like the logical thing to do," he answered with ease. "I would have pulled it off too, if you and your sisters hadn't seen me out for one of my midnight strolls. I had to get out and walk because of the arthritis. Doctor's orders."

"*Doctor?*" Stevie repeated. She cursed under her breath. "George, you're a piece of work. I don't know how any woman ever put up with you."

"Maybe they didn't," I said.

George's ghost smirked as he disappeared and reappeared on the other side of the bedroom.

"Y'all better scoot unless you want to get caught." With a chuckle, George disappeared for good as the sound of a nearby door slamming filled the bedroom. Someone had entered the suite. The five of us sprinted back to the closet.

Despite her claustrophobia, Rickiah was the first one to step back into the secret passageway. She was followed by Junior. Thad nudged me into the wall next and pulled Stevie into the closet, shutting the door just as giggling filled the bedroom. From a crack in the door, we watched Jonathon Carmichael and two women from the party stumble toward the bed. It was obvious that the three of them were intoxicated.

"Mama would definitely not approve of this," Jonathon chided. The two women giggled some more.

I entered the passageway, and Thad followed right behind me. Stevie was the last one to step through. She closed the hidden door as best she could, but the sound of laughter and Jonathon's ill attempts to sound sexy still rang through the walls.

"Gross," Stevie muttered. "Get me out of here before I hear any more of this."

"He should keep his mouth shut." Rickiah's voice floated to the back of the line. Her cell phone lit the cramped staircase that would take us back to the main level. "I mean the dude is rich."

"So, rich people don't have feelings?" Junior teased.

"You know what I mean," Rickiah muttered.

"I don't know why some people are impressed by money," Stevie added. "I'm definitely not."

"Then what *does* impress you?" Junior's comment was quick and casual, and it brought a smile to my face.

"Yeah, Stevie," Thad added. His hand brushed against my elbow. "Lay it on us."

"Find George's mistress and figure out how one of my cheesecakes ended up in Room 111," Stevie replied. "Then I'll tell y'all anything you want to know."

The five of us walked carefully back to the first floor and decided to exit the hotel rather than risk being seen at the crime scene. We'd gotten far enough undetected, and I wanted to make sure things stayed that way.

"Solve the case and win Stevie's heart," Junior joked, although the rest of us knew he wasn't joking at all. "Noted."

My thoughts turned to my nephew, Orion, and Stevie's inner torment over his father. I wasn't sure Stevie had a heart to give away—at least, not a full one. But if I'd learned anything from George Carmichael, it was that a person's heart could be in more than one place at a time.

It could be several places and maybe even with several people.

Chapter 14

After a text from Aqua telling me she wasn't ready to leave the party, I decided I'd definitely had enough for the night. The crowd of protestors camped out on the front steps confirmed it. They'd finally stopped their chanting, reserving all of their energy for unlucky partygoers exiting the Mardi Gras festivities through the front doors. Booing filled the night as a couple strutted outside and handed a valet their ticket.

The five of us bypassed the booing by walking around the side of the hotel and down the hill toward town. Sounds from the Crystal Grande faded as we neared Main Street. The sky was still dark, and clouds overhead covered most of the stars. Streetlights lit the sidewalks, and the sound of heels clattered in my ears. I'd worn heels enough at my old job that I'd learned how to walk at a normal pace while wearing them. The key was ignoring the pain in my feet and propelling my thighs forward with every step. Stevie and Rickiah weren't as well practiced, especially not on pavement.

"Whoa, what a night." Rickiah walked ahead, and I prayed she wouldn't make an awkward joke about being a fifth wheel. "I have to thank y'all for making my life the opposite of boring."

"You're welcome," Stevie replied.

"I'm sorry good ole George wasn't more helpful." Rickiah shook her head. "But I have to say, I saw that one coming."

"Unless he was telling the truth, and he really didn't see who brought the cheesecake," I commented. "He said he sat down, drank his coffee, and then that was it."

"Did he seem like he was telling truth?" Thad stayed close to me, and I didn't mind. It was too dark for him to notice the rosy shade of my cheeks or the fact that my forehead was warm and even a little sweaty.

I took a deep breath. I wanted to think I was good at picking out liars. Sometimes I was, but sometimes liars were really good at lying. I shrugged. Part of me had believed him, especially since he'd admitted to having a mistress even though he hadn't given us a name.

"I think so," I answered. "I mean, is it too far-fetched to think that someone came into the room after George died and staged the crime scene with the red velvet cheesecake?"

"No." Thad's voice was steady and comforting. "We don't know who knows about that secret passageway. Anyone could have used it. The killer could've gone into the room and left without ever walking through the hotel lobby. That passageway changes everything."

"So, we're back to square one." Stevie ran her fingers through her midnight locks and tugged the hem of her dress as she walked. "I guess we need to focus on what got us into this mess in the first place—that freakin' red velvet cheesecake."

"I'll visit Cindy first thing tomorrow," I said.

"You know, when all of this blows over..." Junior inched closer to Stevie, and she folded her arms.

I covered my mouth, wondering if I was about to witness an attempt at asking Stevie out. I couldn't believe he had the guts to do it in front of all of us. Then again, maybe that was part of his vampire charm. My eyes went wide.

Thad stopped suddenly and scanned the street.

"Hold on," he whispered, sniffing the air.

I balled my hands into fists.

Stevie, Junior, and Rickiah, who hadn't heard Thad, were a block ahead of us before they finally stopped too and looked back at us.

Thad peered down a neighboring street and pointed just as a figure jogged out of view. I frowned. It was Friday night, and most of the town was celebrating. There was no need to slither along the streets unseen.

Unless something illegal was involved.

"Who was that?" I muttered. "Did you see his face?"

Thad shook his head and jogged across the street, following the shadow's path. I scanned the road and then followed him, doing my best not to make noise. My goal was impossible to attain. Thad continued to follow the scent he'd picked up in the wind, and it wasn't long before he too disappeared around a corner.

Junior looked ahead and then glanced back at Stevie as if debating whether to follow him or stay.

"We're right behind you." Rickiah urged him to join Thad. The other three had caught up to me by then.

As Junior ran to catch up to Thad, the three of us walked closer to the town square.

"Look at us," Stevie murmured. "We're like sitting ducks in stilettos." She took off her shoes and quickened her pace. Stevie looked over her shoulder. "Well, are you Alabamians or aren't you?"

I grinned, remembering the comments I'd gotten after moving to New York City and telling people where I was from. I'd hated the southern stereotypes, mainly the one that southerners were small-town hicks who ran around barefoot. It hadn't taken long for me to stop telling people about my hometown altogether. In fact, most of my coworkers had been happy to talk about themselves instead, so I'd let them.

The stereotypes didn't bother me as much anymore.

I laughed out loud as my feet hit the sidewalk. Rickiah rolled her eyes as she joined in.

"Do you have any idea how many germs there are out here?" Rickiah stared down at the ground, muttering the comment to herself.

"Over there." Stevie stopped and pointed to a corner across the street where Thad and Junior stood still.

The three of us ran to meet them without disrupting the evening silence.

Thad peered at a mysterious figure down the street—a hooded stranger.

"Wait a minute," Stevie whispered. "That looks like..."

"Kalen?" I wrinkled my nose.

Kalen rubbed a hand over his hood and pulled something from his pocket. He'd stopped in front of a souvenir shop with potted plants at the entrance. Kalen gently slipped something between the leaves and flowers and casually walked away. I waited until he'd turned a corner to investigate.

Stevie was first on the scene. She narrowed her eyes, digging through the plant until she found the item Kalen had hidden. She held it up to the light and frowned.

"Oh, you've got to be kidding me," Stevie stated.

She held a plastic bag in front of her face, and inside the bag was a single cookie.

"Um-hmm." Rickiah chuckled.

"So this is why he asks so many questions." Stevie shook her head and carefully opened the plastic bag. She studied the cookie, sniffing it and feeling the texture. "Plain chocolate chip, huh. How original." Stevie broke the cookie in half and took a small bite.

"Um, Stevie..." The instant she started chewing I realized she'd misread the situation. There was only one reason Kalen would have made the trek to hide a single chocolate chip cookie in the dead of night.

"It tastes OK," she went on, critiquing it. "Could use less baking soda and maybe more sugar." Stevie took another bite. Before I knew it, she'd eaten half the cookie.

Rickiah covered her mouth.

Thad scratched the side of his chin and Junior watched in amusement.

"Stevie," I said, grabbing the cookie. "You might want to stop that."

"Hang on." She snatched the cookie away from me. "I'm not done."

"Psychics party hard," Junior commented. "I had no idea."

"What are you talking about?" Stevie studied the cookie with a look of confusion on her face.

"Oh, sweetie," Rickiah chimed in. "Please tell me you're not that naive." She rubbed her eyes, and then studied Stevie again before letting out a high-pitched laugh.

"Rude." Stevie glared at her and took another bite of the cookie.

"Stevie," I said, my chest pounding. "Kalen left that cookie there for a reason."

"I know." Stevie stamped her foot. "That little brat is opening a bakery of his own. I wonder how many of our recipes he's already stolen."

Rickiah laughed again.

"No, he isn't," I firmly responded. "He's perfecting his baking skills and selling those things for lots of cash."

"It's a cookie." Stevie shrugged.

"Yeah, it's a *special* cookie, Stevie." I grabbed what was left of it and tossed it back in its plastic bag. "I'm sorry. I thought it was obvious."

"Y'all are acting really strange," Stevie argued.

"Stevie, that's an edible." Rickiah had a hard time containing her laughter, and it was starting to piss Stevie off. "You know, cannabis? You just ate half a pot cookie."

Stevie spit what was left in her mouth onto the street.

"What? I'm going to kill all y'all!"

"You better jump on it then," Rickiah replied with a giant grin. "You'll be too relaxed to care in an hour."

Chapter 15

Stevie hadn't been late for work in years.

The last time was due to a terrible stomach bug that forced her to lock herself in the bathroom for hours. The bakery had closed that day.

Saturday morning had arrived, and unlike Stevie, I hadn't gotten a wink of sleep. Thad had helped me get Stevie into the house without waking up my mom and nephew. She'd gone on one of her rants blaming me for letting her eat edibles and explaining how she hadn't used drugs of any kind since high school because they messed with her ability to see the dead. Her rant had ended with her head hitting her pillow and her falling right to sleep.

I'd woken up at six o'clock, and Stevie had still been asleep.

Normally, she left the house around four in the morning and already had fresh batches of morning pastries ready when I walked into the office with Yogi by my side. Trying to wake her up had been like trying to wake the dead. Impossible. She'd been forced to relax for a short evening, and her body had taken full advantage. She must have really needed the rest.

"It's simple." Aqua scratched her head. She'd pulled her hair up in a loose bun and was sipping on her second espresso. Yogi sat by my feet and Whiskers had tagged along for fun. The bakery was supposed to open in an hour, and we had nothing to serve besides yesterday's leftovers. "She keeps the recipes over there, and she keeps dough in the fridge."

Aqua groaned as she stared at the countertops.

"This is what happens when you drink too much," I commented. "We adults still have to work in the morning. Plan better next time."

"No, this is what happens when your big sister doesn't do her job because she ingested too much weed the night before," Aqua corrected me.

"Keep that to yourself." I took a deep breath and glanced up at the fire alarms and sprinklers. My biggest fear was that I'd burn the place down while trying to play Head Baker. "We don't want Mom to have a heart attack."

"Yes, heaven forbid her society ladies find out about it." Aqua rolled her eyes the same way Stevie did. "Did you hear how loud her snoring got last night? I bet she planned this."

"Definitely not. You should have seen her face." I was ready to leave the *Closed* sign up for the day, but I knew that would have made Stevie even madder. I had to at least try. I wasn't *that* helpless.

"So, Kalen is peddling special cookies, huh?" Aqua rubbed at last night's makeup. "I didn't think he had the guts to do something like that. Was it any good?"

"I didn't try it," I responded. "You shouldn't either. They're not legal here. Don't mess up your chances of transferring to a four-year university.

Besides, you'll learn fast that drugs and sometimes even alcohol can mess with your psychic gift."

"I can't figure that fur ball out with or without bourbon." She pointed to Whiskers, and he looked up at her. "What? Now you want to talk?" She paused and then rubbed her forehead in frustration. "See? Still nothing."

"And Yogi?"

"He's already thinking about his next meal." A slight smile crossed Aqua's face as she glanced at the hound. "He's just as predictable as Dad was—a creature of habit."

"I imagine most dogs are."

"Yeah, maybe cats are just a whole 'nother—"

"*Animal?*" I finished.

"Any news from Nova?" Aqua asked. "Did we really just add a witch's familiar to our family lineup? Because I'm pretty sure that has never been done before."

"For the time being." I shrugged and rolled up my sleeves.

I had no idea where to start, and so I began my hour of fearful baking by looking in the fridge. I was relieved to find it fully stocked, but I didn't know what was what. Balls of dough were neatly wrapped in plastic, and tubs of different fillings and frostings sat on the shelf below. The tubs had been labeled, but the doughs weren't.

"Start with croissants," Aqua suggested. "All we have to do is roll them up. Oh, and pull out the cookie doughs. Everyone loves cookies. Stevie included." She smirked and began retrieving baking pans.

"Which one is the croissant dough?" I had too many options.

"Uh..." Aqua joined me at the fridge and shrugged. "If I had to guess...umm..."

"You work here, Aqua. Do you really not know?"

"Hey, I mostly make the coffees, OK?" She held her hands up. "I'm an expert at the register but not kitchen stuff. That's Stevie's domain."

"We really need an assistant," I muttered. "OK." I sighed. "I'll just make an educated guess."

"Based on what?" Aqua cleared her throat, her mischievous smirk returning. "Decades of culinary experience?"

"Haha." I eyed each ball of dough and touched one in the middle. "Maybe this one?"

Whiskers meowed from the top of the fridge, and I jumped back with a loud yelp. He'd appeared out of nowhere, and he stared at me until I gave him my full attention. My heart pounded, and Yogi rushed to my aid. He barked at Whiskers until the cat hissed back.

I patted the top of Yogi's head and waited for him to settle down. Whiskers watched me like a hawk as I reached for the dough in the fridge a second time. I touched the same round ball on the center of the shelf. Whiskers jumped onto my arm and touched a ball of dough to my left. Whiskers glanced back at me, and then touched the same ball of dough again.

I raised my eyebrows.

"Get that cat out of the fridge," Aqua ordered.

"I think he's..." I grabbed the ball of dough Whiskers had picked and he purred. "OK." I handed it to Aqua. "Does this look like croissant dough?"

She shrugged. "I guess we'll soon find out, won't we?"

Whiskers jumped out of my arms and fixated on the two of us as we unwrapped the dough and prepared to roll it out and cut it into triangles. We planned on making a few pans of plain croissants and a few pans with chocolate—Aqua's personal bakery favorite. As soon as the batch of croissants went into the oven, it was clear that I'd picked the right dough.

Aqua baked an assortment of cookies using the premade doughs Stevie had previously prepared, and I moved on to stocking the display case in front with day-old pound cake, muffins, and a few Danishes. The bakery was finally starting to look and smell the way it normally did when it opened in the morning.

"We might have to delay opening our doors for another hour." I glanced at the time. We weren't completely ready for customers, but an hour late was better than not opening at all. Especially on a Saturday, when there was prime tourist traffic and Main Street was crowded because of the Mardi Gras celebrations going on at the Crystal Grande. That included the first parade of many happening just before lunch.

"We can't," Aqua responded. "There are like a dozen king cakes in the fridge that are supposed to be picked up this morning. Not to mention, we should be making more."

"Sorry, Stevie," I muttered under my breath. "Fine. We'll open on time. What should we do about the donuts?"

"I can do the Mardi Gras glaze Stevie showed me last week, but the frying?" She twisted her lips, her eyes darting to the large fryer Stevie had just bought.

"Well, don't look at me," I commented. "A toaster and a microwave is as brave as I get." I took a deep breath and headed to my office. I called Stevie's cell phone. No answer. I shook my head and dialed the house phone, knowing my mom would answer. She was the only one of us who still used a landline.

"Hello, Greene residence?" The sound of my mom's voice gave me hope.

"Mom, this is Ember," I answered. "Please tell me that Stevie is awake."

"Stevie isn't with you?"

"Well..." I gulped. I didn't like lying to my mother, but Aqua and I were getting desperate. And we couldn't close the bakery during the upcoming parade. It was sure to bring in a ton of business. We needed business. "We stayed out late last night, and Stevie decided to sleep in."

"Sleep in?" she repeated. "But the parades start today."

Crap. She's not buying it.

"Aqua and I have it covered," I lied.

"Then why are you calling, honey?"

"Because . . ." I took a deep breath. "Look, is Stevie awake? Can't you just check on her for me?"

"All right," my mom agreed. "But whatever you're hiding, I'll figure it out. It's just a matter of time."

"Yep. I know."

She hung up.

"Well?" Aqua leaned in the doorframe and tilted her head. "Is Stevie going to grace us with her presence?"

"That's a toss-up."

The two of us stepped back into the kitchen and took the croissants out of the oven. They looked close to Stevie's. Aqua tasted one we'd filled with chocolate and gave it her nod of approval. I eyed the fryer again. Maybe we weren't the worst bakers in the world.

"Luann will be here any minute. I'll let her run the register while we move on to the cakes." Aqua untied her apron and headed into the café to set up chairs.

I opened the fridge, searching for the dough Stevie used for donuts. Before I could take a guess, Whiskers appeared again and jumped into my arms. This time I held him toward the shelf, and his paw rested gently on a ball of dough. I grabbed the dough and unwrapped it on the counter.

"Maybe the Grants and the Hextons were wrong about you, Whiskers," I observed as he stared up at me, his big yellow eyes like two full moons watching my every move. "There's something different about you. You must have some sort of magical gift, and eventually I'll figure out what it is."

Whiskers meowed in response, and Yogi added a short bark to the conversation.

"You're special too, Yogi," I added.

I read and reread Stevie's donut recipe a hundred times before getting up the courage to turn on the fryer. Stevie had already done the hard part. The dough was ready. I was worried about getting the donuts to that golden brown color.

The bell above the door chimed as customers trickled in. I heard the sound of chatter, laughter, and coffee cups on the counter. A pressure built up behind my eyes as I looked at the donut recipe again and reviewed the frying instructions.

"Should I put the fire department on standby?" The familiar voice drifted into the kitchen.

Yogi wagged his tail uncontrollably as my mom entered the room and threw on an apron.

"Oh, thank the cosmos," I muttered. A wave of relief rushed over me.

"I know I haven't been at the bakery as much after your father passed, but I did use to run this place when you were little." She checked the fryer. "Of course, our equipment wasn't this fancy, and I had help in the kitchen back then."

"About Stevie—"

"She's still conked out in her room," Mom said. "Orion is in the café with a snack, and my knees are feeling good today. I don't know what happened last night, but your sister has needed a morning like this for years. Maybe she'll get so much rest that she'll wake up a different person."

"If it's a person who isn't mad at me all the time then I'm OK with that," I responded.

Mom took the lead and helped me finish the rest of the baking. Her donuts came out of the fryer a perfect shade of golden brown, and Aqua was ready with the Mardi Gras decorations. We sold out in less than an hour, and business boomed when the sound of drums and trumpets took over Main Street.

All of our customers moved to the front windows. I joined Orion and my mom just outside the entrance as the first float came into view. It had a giant purple mask on the front and dozens of shimmery decorations. Onlookers clapped as the marching band from Misty Key High School followed behind it.

"Granny, look." A huge smile spread across Orion's face. He pointed to a float that had been designed to look like an alligator gliding through the streets. Beads of every color were hanging from its mouth, and a tiny gold crown sat on top of its head. Next to the golden crown, a woman danced. She wore a sparkly bra and matching bottoms that sat at her hips.

"Good gracious," Mom muttered, covering her mouth as she gasped. "Is there anything that woman won't do for attention?"

"Granny, I meant the gator," Orion added with a giggle.

"Well, good." She lifted her chin. "You just keep your innocent eyes off of that tramp up there...bless her heart."

My mom turned around and walked straight back inside the bakery.

The alligator float passed by us, and the woman on top continued dancing.

It was Cindy Buford—a student and a suspect.

Chapter 16

The bakery had closed, and there was still no sign of Stevie.

The good news was we'd been able to make it through the day without her thanks to her kitchen organization skills. The bad news was that we really needed a baking assistant because our baked goods still weren't as magical as Stevie's. A couple of our regulars had noticed.

Mom locked the doors and walked back to the house with Aqua and Orion, and I headed into town to have a chat with Cindy. Yogi stuck to my side, and Whiskers lingered behind us, stopping at every corner before running to catch up. As long as he stayed out of the street, I didn't mind him following me anymore.

The parade had ended at the Pelican Playhouse. It had been an old Italian restaurant before it was turned into a small theatre. It had served as a home base for Mardi Gras celebrations for years, and I didn't doubt that Cindy would be there getting ready for her next performance. Cindy owned the place.

Floats were parked outside of the playhouse and around back. Some of them were guarded by their creators, and some of them were empty. I pushed past the hustle and bustle and went in through the front entrance. The lobby area was small, with red carpet and wallpaper that looked like old-fashioned bricks.

There was just enough room to wait in line at the ticket office and not much else.

Past the ticket office were doors leading into the theatre. I let myself in and waited for Yogi and Whiskers to enter the building before closing the door behind me. There were three levels comprised of various tables and chairs with the main stage at the bottom. The walls and floors were black. Even with the lights on, the room was still dark.

The exception was the stage.

The red velvet curtains were open, revealing backstage props and equipment. Lights twinkled and lit up center stage where Cindy stood practicing her dance routine. She'd changed out of her Mardi Gras bra and matching bottoms and was wearing a tank top and tight leggings. Her blonde curls fell over her face as she danced, paying little attention to me and my furry entourage as we approached her.

"See you outside, Cindy." A man wearing sunglasses and a Hawaiian shirt stepped off of the stage and headed for the exit.

"See you, Don." Her southern accent flowed out of her mouth like honey, making her seem much more innocent than I knew she was. Cindy finally concentrated on something other than the center stage. "Oh, hello. What brings you here?"

"Hi, Cindy." I lifted myself up onto the stage. Yogi jumped up after me, followed by Whiskers. Cindy immediately knelt down and stroked Whiskers until he purred.

"What a gorgeous kitty." Cindy held Whiskers in her arms. "I hope you're not here to complain."

"Complain about what?" I asked as another parade participant emerged from backstage and headed outside with a friendly wave.

"My float." Cindy rolled her eyes. "Of course Mary Jean had something to say about it, but I don't care. The next parade starts soon, and I have to get dressed." She walked farther backstage, letting go of Whiskers.

"I saw your performance," I admitted. "Your float was very impressive. My little nephew loved the alligator."

"From New Orleans with love." Cindy beamed and kept walking. She dragged her fingers across a piano, maneuvered around a table with feathery masks, and strode right into a dressing room with her name on the door.

"I came to ask you about the baking course," I continued.

"*Now?*" She studied me suspiciously as I leaned in the door frame. I nodded and Yogi barked in agreement. "Come on in. You can talk while I change."

I entered her dressing room, not surprised by its size and décor. It was bigger than my bedroom. There was a full-length mirror against one wall and a vanity against another. Bottles of perfume and makeup covered the surface, and a rack of glittery clothing stood next to an antique couch that added an old Hollywood feel to the space.

"Nice place," I said. I cleared my throat and steered Yogi away from the antique couch.

"I got that couch at Mrs. Johnston's. It came all the way from Brentwood. It's worth a fortune." Cindy didn't even blush as she pulled the tank top over her head, taking care not to ruin her curls. I quickly turned away. "My apologies if you aren't comfortable with showing a little skin." I saw her search for her top through the mirror.

"You be you," I commented. "Trust me, I don't judge. My life is way too messy."

"I know what the other society ladies say about me," Cindy went on. "None of it's true."

"So, you don't go for morning swims in the nude?" I grinned, remembering my mom discussing Cindy's inappropriate exercise routines over dinner one night.

"Oh, well, that one is true." Cindy finally found her clothes and threw them on. "But there's no law against being naked on my own property."

"Um, I think that's debatable once you step outside."

"I'm talking about the money. I have plenty of it, and I don't need a man to support myself." Cindy talked over me, and I continued facing the wall and using my leg to block Yogi from sniffing the couch some more. If he decided to take a taste of it, I didn't have the cash to replace it.

"I don't pay attention to that stuff," I admitted. And it was true. The rumors were out there. She'd been married six times, and there were whispers that she was on the hunt for a seventh, but I didn't waste my time with the details.

"Well, you're sweet." Cindy took a deep breath and studied her reflection. She flexed her abs. Her Mardi Gras costume left little to the imagination, and from far away, no one would have guessed she was in her fifties. "You're also a working woman. You don't have time to entertain the gossipers. Some women in this town need a hobby."

Cindy pulled the skin around her belly button and frowned.

"Is this a bad time to ask you about that red velvet cheesecake you made in class?" I asked.

Cindy stepped closer to the mirror and played with the skin around her eyes.

"Getting old is inevitable," she muttered. "But I still hate it. One day you'll get it."

"I think you look great for—"

"For a woman in her fifties?" Cindy raised her eyebrows. "My dear, that's an insult in disguise." She adjusted her outfit so that it covered more of her lower abdomen. "My last husband left me for a twenty-five-year-old. How old are you?" Her eyes darted to my eyes as if the creases around my eyelids would give it away.

"I'm older than that, Cindy."

"Hmm." Cindy grabbed a bottle of lotion and began lathering her legs with an orange-scented cream.

"Do you still have the cheesecake you made on Monday?"

"As a matter of fact, I do," she answered. "It's at home in the fridge. I'd invite you over but I'm rather busy. Also, I don't think Leila would approve."

"My mom is just...well, she's been through a lot lately," I tried to explain.

"I know." Cindy rubbed more lotion on her arms. "I've given her a free pass since Steven died. Your father was a good man. He was always very kind to me."

"Yes, he was." I sighed.

"If you don't mind, I need to get to my float." Cindy rubbed her hands together and took one last look in the mirror. She winked at her reflection, satisfied with her appearance, and marched out of her dressing room and back on stage. She looked over her shoulder. "Is that really what you came here to ask me?"

"Uh, I guess the rest can wait for another time," I said, although it was. The mystery of the red velvet cheesecake was becoming harder and harder to solve. I also didn't know how Stevie's students would react if I forced my way into their houses and demanded to see the red velvet cheesecake crumbs. That would kill enrollment for Stevie's baking course.

"There's something strange about you Greene women." Cindy paused for a moment and stared down at Whiskers. She touched the side of her cheek with her pointer finger. "I swear one of these days I'll figure it out."

"Strange?" I forced a laugh that didn't come out sounding natural at all.

"Yes."

My uncomfortable chuckle had only added to her suspicions, because she fixated on my caramel hair and rosy cheeks.

"Good luck with the parade." I did my best to change the subject before I trudged too far down an uncharted path. "I'll make sure I buy tickets to your next play."

"My last one sold out fast," Cindy commented. Her smile returned in a heartbeat at the mention of her latest theatrics. "Of course, the *Misty Messenger* chalked it up to one of my outfits. A sheer little number that looked just fine during rehearsals."

"I'm sure it was your talented cast that drew in customers," I replied.

"That's exactly what I said." Cindy twirled her curls. "I gave a quote to the papers, and they didn't even publish it."

"What matters is that you sold out."

"Yes, Ember, you're exactly right."

Cindy held her head high and hopped off the stage. I followed her back through the theatre and toward the tiny lobby at the front of the building. Yogi pushed the side of my calf with his nose while Whiskers ran along in front of us.

Before we got to the main entrance, Cindy stopped and turned around.

"Did you forget something?" I asked.

"I was just thinking..." She checked the time. "Oh my, I'm already late, but I was thinking you would be perfect for our upcoming production of *Marigold Is*

Misbehavin'. You should come and audition next week."

I wrinkled my nose. "I'm not an actress. Believe me. You'd be better off picking someone else."

"Are you sure, because—"

BOOM.

The entire building shook.

The sudden noise tore through the theatre and made my blood pump so fast my hands shook. I balled my sweaty palms into fists as Whiskers jumped into my arms and Yogi stepped in front of me growling. Cindy had dropped to the floor, her eyes wide with shock.

A few seconds of silence filled the room.

I had goose bumps.

I searched my surroundings, terrified of what I might see.

A few lights had crashed onto the stage, but that was about it.

I tried to steady my breathing.

But that didn't work.

Because next came the sound of screaming from outside.

Chapter 17

Time had never been a friend of mine.

It seemed to stand still when I didn't want it to and speed up when I needed as much time as I could get. Time sped buy in a whirlwind of chaos as I stepped outside the Pelican Playhouse and witnessed a pandemonium that was difficult to describe. Cindy was at my heels, and she fell over the moment she saw flames.

Yogi barked, and I did my best to keep her from passing out.

People crowded the street.

There was more screaming than I could handle.

And at the center of it all was a burst of heat that sent tingles through my hands and feet.

"My floats," Cindy finally cried. "My beautiful, beautiful floats!"

Tears filled her cheeks as she observed the nearest cluster of flames devouring a parade float. Sirens filled the air, and I yanked Cindy away before she could walk closer to the damage. A man shouted for everyone to get as far away from the theatre as possible just as another loud *boom* sounded on the street.

Cindy and I dropped to the pavement, my ears ringing. Chunks of plywood and rogue beads dropped to the ground on both sides of us. I instinctively covered my head. Cindy looked right past me and screamed.

A giant alligator head lay in pieces.

Cindy's float had been destroyed.

"Cindy, just calm down." My voice was shaky, but I forced myself to appear cool and collected even though I was freaking out just as much as she was beneath the surface. "We need to get out of here."

"It's those evil protestors!" Cindy shouted. "They did this. I'll prove it, and they'll pay!"

Police cars stopped down the street, and officers filled the area, escorting people to safety left and right. An ambulance stopped near the injured, and a team of medics began assessing the scene. Yogi nudged me, and I followed the rest of the crowd, pulling Cindy with me. Whiskers clung to my shoulder, digging his claws into my emerald green blouse. I would probably never be able to repair the rips.

"Come on." I dragged Cindy farther down the street.

She stopped and took a breath, wiping away the makeup dripping down her face.

"I just...I can't believe this," she uttered in between sniffles.

I shook my head.

From far away, it was easy to guess what had happened. Parade floats were in pieces, and the fire department was working to extinguish the last of the flames. It couldn't have been an accident. Someone was responsible.

Cindy's alligator float had been a target.

"Cindy, take a deep breath," I said. "Can you think of anyone who might want to harm you?"

"What?" Her chest heaved and she pulled at the straps of her top. "I think I'm going to have a panic attack." Her breathing quickened even more. "Oh, no. No. This can't be happening. No. Oh, no."

"Just breathe."

"Ember, if you tell me to *breathe* one more time, so help me..." She closed her eyes and clutched her sides. "This isn't real. I must be dreaming." Cindy squeezed her eyes even tighter. "Yes. This is a dream. A horrible nightmare. And when I count to ten, I'll be home under my pink comforter."

"Uh, Cindy?"

"Just a dream," she repeated. "Dreams. Dreams. Dreams."

"Cindy, can you hear me?" I went on. "Has anything odd happened to you lately? Weird phone calls? Threats? Maybe a letter in the mail?"

With a huff, Cindy opened her eyes. Her nostrils flared when her gaze darted to the mess of parade floats in front of us.

"Shoot. You're still here." Cindy rubbed her eyes.

"I'm only trying to help, here."

"By asking me if I've checked my mailbox lately?" Cindy replied.

"Hey, you said yourself that you were running late," I pointed out. "Your float exploded, and *you* were supposed to be on it."

She hunched her shoulders and looked down at the pavement.

"If that's true then I suggest you butt out." Her eyes narrowed, and her panicked expression suddenly turned cold.

"I want to help," I insisted.

"I hope this isn't the real reason you came here to see me." She glared in my direction. "Butt out or you'll be next."

Chapter 18

"Is revenge still on your mind?"

I watched Stevie sip a cup of sweet tea at the kitchen table. She hadn't scowled at me once, and a smile had been permanently ingrained on her face since entering the kitchen. Orion sat next to her with a plate of half-eaten dinner, and Aqua stood at the kitchen counter helping my mom light a few of her evening candles.

"A lot of things are on my mind, Ember," she quietly replied.

Her new demeanor creeped me out. Mostly because I had no idea when the real Stevie would return and fly off the handle over something stupid like cookie crumbs on the counter.

"Ember, sit down and have some sweet chicken salad," Mom instructed.

"I don't have much of an appetite right now," I muttered.

News of the explosion was already common knowledge around Misty Key. For one, the evening Mardi Gras parade had been canceled due to technical difficulties, and Cindy had insisted on the local news that the incident was all a mistake. The Pelican Playhouse was a safe environment, and though some people had been injured, no one was in critical condition.

Everyone had been lucky.

"Someone must be after Auntie again," Orion muttered. His shiny black hair was tangled, and his bright blue eyes narrowed much like his mother's did when she made snide comments.

"Someone always is." Stevie chuckled along with her son.

"Aw, look at you two." Aqua tilted her head, her cell phone in one hand. "Laughing and teasing together like normal families do."

Whiskers strolled into the kitchen with Yogi. The two of them stopped at the kitchen table right next to Orion. It wasn't long before Yogi showcased his usual begging face, hoping Orion would toss him an extra scrap. Sometimes he did, because Yogi ate vegetables. To him, food was food, as Aqua had put it.

Some of my anxieties faded as I observed the way Whiskers copied him.

"You know I'm not allowed, Yogi." Orion scooted closer to Stevie.

"Looks like those two are friends now," Aqua pointed out.

"At the moment anyway," my mom added. "You know how cats and dogs can get."

"Maybe he'll eat Whiskers for lunch one of these days," Orion added. "That would be cool."

"Orion, that's disgusting." Aqua watched Stevie, who had always been quick to scold her son whenever he talked about death and bodily fluids.

Stevie just cracked a smile.

A knock at the front door grabbed my attention. Yogi's head turned, my mom took a whiff of her candles, and I walked into the living room. I wasn't surprised to see Nova on the doorstep. Her oversized purse hung from her shoulder, and her auburn hair was half up, the rest falling past her shoulders, and her yellow and ivory dress reminded me of a lemon meringue pie.

"Please don't tell me we've been assigned a new case." I took a deep breath.

"That would be a hard, fast *no*," she answered, stepping inside. "May I come in? Thank you."

I shut the door as she strolled into the kitchen, knowing that whatever news she had would just add to the stress of our situation. With a permanent grin, Nova set her bag on the kitchen table and sat across from Stevie. She eyed Yogi and Whiskers.

"I'm sure y'all are wondering what this is about," Nova announced.

"Not really," Stevie murmured into her cup. She and Orion both giggled.

"I've just been to Cottonberry, per the Grant family's request," she explained. "Apparently, they are very unhappy with how the mediation turned out and they've filed a WRR-2 with Wisteria, Inc."

"Of course they did." I crossed my arms, securing a spot along the kitchen counter next to my mom. I studied Stevie's expression. It was strange to talk about Cottonberry and the Grant family without a single scowl or sarcastic comment from her. Apparently she was too well-rested for that.

"Uh, what's that?" Aqua pulled a strand of her hair.

"It's a reversal request," Nova replied. "To put it plainly, they want a do-over with a new set of Seers."

"That's rude." Aqua bit the side of her lip. "Are they just going to keep on asking for re-dos until they find Seers they like?"

"Seers they can bribe is more like it," I commented.

"A Seer would *never* take a bribe." Nova lifted her chin and straightened her shoulders, a firm tone emitting from her lips. "It's against the oath. And Wisteria, Inc. denied their request. That's what I came to tell you. Whiskers is yours free and clear."

"Seriously?" I tilted my head, remembering the winnowing ceremony and the look in Whiskers's eyes when he'd chosen me. "A psychic family with a familiar? Is that even a thing? What are we supposed to do with him?"

"There's a first time for everything, right?" Nova glanced at Yogi. "I thought y'all would be happy since you clearly like animals. And it's another chance for Aqua to practice her talent."

"Right." Aqua's eyes darted around the room and her cheeks went rosy. "Maybe we should talk about that."

"You can communicate with, um…" Nova pointed at Yogi with her chin, a look of apprehension spreading across her face.

"Yogi," Stevie chimed in. "His name is Yogi." She nudged Orion. "Nova's more of a cat person. You should see the Siamese that follows her around."

Nova's eyes went wide.

"Siamese?" she repeated.

I'd known about the ghost cat since I'd first met Nova. Stevie had mentioned it several times, and Yogi had even barked at the feline on more than one occasion. But Stevie had never mentioned it to Nova until now.

"Yeah, you don't know?" Stevie shrugged. It seemed that her relaxed state had also made her a little insensitive because she ignored the unsettled expression on Nova's face and went back to sipping her tea. "Ma, will you hand me the sugar jar?"

"Excuse me." Nova stood up and clutched the straps of her purse. "I need to go."

"Nova, she didn't mean to be so blunt," my mom clarified. "We all lose loved ones, pets included."

"Thank you, Leila." Nova smiled at her. "But I really do need to go."

With one long exhale, Nova regained her sense of professionalism and opened her bag. She pulled out a small package that fit into the palm of her hand and placed it next to Stevie. I snuck a glimpse over Stevie's shoulder and saw Stevie's name on it.

"What's this?" Stevie touched the package, searching for a clue about the sender. The package had no return address.

"A man named Warner wanted you to have it," Nova answered.

Stevie's hand immediately recoiled.

"What did he say?" Her voice was steady, but I knew there was a thunderstorm brewing beneath the surface. Her confrontation with Warner was still fresh in my mind.

"He happened to be visiting his mother when I stopped by," Nova said. "He asked me if I would give this to you. He said it was important, and he told me to tell you to at least open it."

"If that thing is from Cottonberry she'll probably toss it in the trash," Aqua muttered.

"That's her choice." Nova took a deep breath, patted Whiskers on the head, and then headed out the front door.

"Are you going to open it, Mom?" Orion was just as antsy as all of us, and he had no problem saying it.

Stevie glared at the package as if she'd be able to spontaneously light it on fire if she concentrated hard enough.

"Isn't it past your bedtime?" Stevie paused and waited for Orion to put his dirty plate in the sink and reluctantly march upstairs.

"There's the old Stevie we know and love." Aqua chuckled.

"Aqua, make yourself useful and brew a pot of coffee."

"A *what* of coffee?"

"Just do it." Stevie clenched her jaw, and Aqua rolled her eyes. "I have a lot of catching up to do at the bakery. The kitchen better be clean, and I hope none of you messed with the new pantry layout. It took me forever to get everything alphabetized."

I kept an eye on the package on the table.

"Stevie," I said. She turned around. "Do you want me to uh…"

"No," she quietly answered. "I'll deal with it." Mom attended to the dishes in the sink while Aqua searched for a coffee filter. When the sound of running water was loud enough to drown out our whispers, Stevie's shoulders slumped in defeat. "It's probably something expensive to settle his guilty conscience."

"In that case, sell it for extra cash."

"Or I could toss it into the ocean," she replied. "I would rather do that."

* * *

Stevie was back.

She'd insisted on spending her Sunday off at the bakery prepping for the coming week. The package she'd received from Warner Grant sat in my office. I'd found it in the trash and had decided to keep it around just in case Stevie changed her mind. I knew she wouldn't. I would have to convince her to at least open it, and keeping it had seemed like a good idea at the time. But the tiny parcel was like a grenade that could go off at any time. I'd shoved it in a desk drawer.

"I'm impressed that everything still works," Stevie commented as she cut thin slices of butter for her latest batch of croissant dough.

"I even touched the fryer," I added, crossing my arms. "And look, no grease fire."

"There's a word for when you read instructions and then follow them." Stevie's eyes darted to the corner of the room where Whiskers was up on a shelf watching her work from afar. He'd left Yogi to nap in my office and had followed me into the kitchen. "It's called adulting."

"I'll make note of that."

"Is it bad that I'm not looking forward to tomorrow?" Stevie continued.

"You never look forward to Mondays. Not since we started the baking course anyway."

"Almost a week ago, one of *my* students walked out of here with a red velvet cheesecake that might ruin us all." She stopped and took a deep breath. "I'm also ready to strangle Kalen next time I see him."

"You did get some good rest though," I replied. "You have to admit that."

"I don't have to admit anything, Ember." Stevie arranged her croissant dough and grabbed a rolling pin. She glared at Whiskers. "We need to do something about that cat."

"Like what?"

"Like lock him in your bedroom or something," Stevie responded. "He doesn't listen to me the way Yogi does. I'm paranoid he's going to tackle one of my cakes one of these days, not to mention he shouldn't even be in here in the first place."

"I've tried everything, and he still ends up here anyway." I observed the cat's blank expression as he continued to stare at the ingredients on the counter.

"Maybe that's his superpower," Stevie muttered. "I find it hard to believe he doesn't have one. Although the Grants could have been hoarding his talents for themselves."

"Whatever he is, he seems to know a lot about baking," I added, recalling the way he'd jumped into my arms and pointed to the things I'd needed in the fridge.

"Oh, perfect." Stevie didn't bother looking at me. She kept on folding and rolling her dough. "All of our problems have been solved. Why don't we put him in charge then?"

"It's not a joke," I insisted. "Yesterday, he—"

"That's great, Ember." Stevie's tone was a little harsher than usual. It would have offended most people, but I was used to it. She wasn't known for her patience. "I'm kind of in the middle of something, so..."

"Sure," I said. "I'll leave you alone. You don't have to say something offensive to get me to skedaddle like Nova did."

"I hardly think that the mention of a Siamese cat was offensive." Stevie paused again, rolling her eyes.

"You saw Nova's face," I pointed out. "She hides it well, but she was definitely upset."

"She'll get over it."

"Not if the death of her pet was recent," I responded. "We haven't known Nova very long, you know."

Stevie blew out a breath and replied in a snarky tone, "Remind me to apologize next time I see her."

I couldn't stand her sarcasm anymore. With a loud exhale of my own, I turned to head back to the office, but a flashing number on the oven stopped me. At first, I assumed it was a timer Stevie had set. Nothing beeped, and Stevie paid little attention to it.

The number was for me.

My chest pounded, and I pulled out my cell phone just as it started ringing.

"Yes." I answered it quickly as I darted back to the office and shut the door.

"Ember Greene?"

My first thought was that Mr. Cohen had dialed my number to see if I'd made up my mind about his job offer yet.

But the voice on the other end wasn't my old boss.

"Detective," I replied, "I hope you have good news for me."

"I'm afraid not."

My heart sank.

"What?"

"I've been sitting on some test results hoping I wouldn't have to make this phone call," he continued. "The fatal substance in George Carmichael's system matched one that was found in that cheesecake of yours."

"That still doesn't prove that one of *our* cheesecakes killed him," I argued. "I mean, it's a setup. That crime scene was staged. Please tell me you've explored that possibility."

"I've explored all possibilities, Ms. Greene. But I have to consider the facts, and I also have to address them."

"I understand," I said, my voice a little shaky. Yogi opened an eye and perked up as soon as he saw the look on my face. My cheeks were as warm as a batch of Stevie's hot cinnamon buns.

My time was up, and I'd failed to figure out who was behind the murder of George Carmichael.

"I'll be stopping by the bakery with my team today," he explained. "This time we'll be confiscating equipment and ingredients, and running lots of tests."

"Your last search was pretty thorough," I pointed out.

"Well, this time will be even more involved now that we know for sure the cheesecake was poisoned."

"I see."

"And one other thing." His voice softened unexpectedly. "All activity is to be suspended until we've finished our tests."

"I don't understand," I lied. My stomach went sour, and a wave of nausea washed over me. My worst fears were coming true, and I couldn't stop them.

"You have to close the bakery until further notice," he clarified. "I know it's how your family makes a living, but it's protocol. I've given you the benefit of the doubt as long as I possibly could."

"Thanks." It was all I could bring myself to say.

"I'm sorry." Detective Winter hung up, but his words still circled my office and wouldn't stop.

I hadn't uncovered the identity of George's killer, which meant that a psychopath still roamed the streets.

And also, Stevie was going to kill me.

Chapter 19

We'd been defeated.

Stevie was madder than words as we sat outside the Lunar Bakery Monday afternoon while a police team banged around inside. We had a lot of work to do before we reopened, which consisted of rearranging everything and replacing all of our ingredients. Stevie had already shed a tear when she'd watched a police officer empty the fridge and take all of her doughs and fillings to the lab for testing.

"I can't just sit here," Stevie blurted out. "Without the bakery, I don't even know what to do with myself."

The sun shone overhead, and the humid air made it feel like summer was coming. It was the perfect day for more Mardi Gras celebrations, and the Crystal Grande Hotel had already resumed their regularly scheduled events following the float explosions on Saturday. More tourists poured into town the closer it got to Fat Tuesday, and I cringed just thinking about all of the business we would be missing.

"Sorry." I took a deep breath and glanced at Whiskers, who sat at my side. Yogi had chosen to stay home with Aqua.

"Sure." She shook her head.

"I really am."

"Ember, the bakery is all I have." She directed her attention toward me, and I shifted uncomfortably on the sidewalk. "You have like hundreds of other things going for you, but *this* is it for me. I've guarded it with my life and had no problem doing so until you came around and wanted to change everything."

"I'm not having this argument right now." I took a deep breath. No matter what I said, my sister would always blame me if we never reopened our doors.

"Exactly." She lifted her chin as if she'd won. "So don't tell me *sorry* because you can't sympathize and you can't promise me that this will never happen again."

A shadow blocked the ray of sun that had been beating down on my forehead. I looked up and saw Kalen pushing his glasses up the bridge of his nose and squinting at the pair of us. His eyes jumped from the sidewalk and then to the darkened bakery windows. He sniffed the air.

"Y'all are closed?" he asked, frowning. "But what about class? We were supposed to start pastries this week." He adjusted the strap of his backpack, which I guessed held his valet uniform and any special cookies that needed delivering.

"Yep, we've been shut down until further notice." Stevie stood and looked up at him. He was taller than her but lanky enough to shove into the nearest flowerbed.

"This ought to be good," I murmured to Whiskers. He meowed in response.

"But don't tell anyone that," Stevie went on. "If anyone asks, we're doing inventory. You can do that, right? You can lie for us?"

"OK." Kalen's eyes narrowed. "I get the message. I'll see you next week."

"Are those glasses even real?" Stevie couldn't help herself. She took a step toward him before he could be on his way. "I mean, sometimes you wear them and sometimes you don't."

"Ever heard of contacts?" Kalen looked to me for some clarity, but I just shrugged.

"I've heard of quite a few things, Kalen."

Kalen wrinkled his nose.

"All right, see ya."

"Oh, I'm not done," Stevie said, raising her voice even more. "How about you show me what's in that backpack of yours. You know, there are policemen just a holler away."

"Maybe I should give them a call." There was no fear in Kalen's eyes as he barked back at her. "What's the matter with you two?"

"She's pissed at you," I blurted out. "She ate one of your chocolate chip cookies and slept all day."

Kalen's eyes went wide.

"Really?" He cleared his throat. "So, what did you think?"

"Too much baking soda," Stevie answered. "Oh, and too much of some other ingredient I forget the name of...um, *weed* maybe?"

"I can explain." Kalen held his hands up.

"You're skimming *my* recipes to fuel your dirty little business." She hit his shoulder.

"That's not what she thought at first," I added, suppressing a laugh.

"Shut up, Ember."

"Geez." Kalen rubbed his wound. "I thought you of all people would be cool with it, Stevie."

"I have enough problems of my own without your illegal little side hustle originating in *my* bakery," she shouted.

Kalen looked up and down Main Street.

"Keep your voice down, will ya." He lowered his voice and rubbed his scrawny shoulder some more. "It's not illegal in every state."

"Are you planning on moving to Colorado or something?" Stevie placed a hand on her hip.

"As a matter of fact, I am." He nodded proudly. "I want to start a business there. I've been saving up for a year."

Stevie decreased the intensity of her glare. Investing your life's savings was hard enough, and starting a business from scratch was even harder. I knew that firsthand, and so did Stevie. We'd sat around the same kitchen table and had heard the same tales of our parents' struggles to keep food in the house. I snuck a glimpse of the neon *Open* sign in the front window that had been off all day.

The Lunar Bakery had come a long way since it had first opened its doors. The café held memories of birthday parties, heart-to-hearts with my dad, and nights spent doing homework. It provided tasty sweets to all of the residents of Misty Key and local businesses. Even the Crystal Grande depended on it for fresh-baked bread. I couldn't let it shut down forever because of a misunderstanding.

"Fine, Kalen." Stevie sighed. "Just stop recipe testing until the course is over."

"You got it." He grinned, grabbed the strap of his backpack, and then walked off down the street. He paused and turned around before he got too far. "And no charge for the cookie even though you've set me back a pretty penny."

"Get the *kale* out of here before I call your ma!" Stevie waved him off and rubbed her temples.

Whiskers meowed, and my eyes darted to the license plate of a passing car. Three numbers flashed before me—calling to me like I was their only hope at delivering their message from the universe. A knot formed at the pit of my stomach as I looked across the street and saw Cindy walking briskly toward a restaurant on the corner.

I'd seen three fours.

I really hate fours.

Seeing three of them together was incredibly unlucky.

I ignored the annoyed look on Stevie's face as I ran across the street and jogged to catch up with Cindy.

Maybe all wasn't lost after all.

"Cindy," I said, catching my breath as best as I could. "Hey, Cindy."

"Oh, it's you." She raised an eyebrow and continued walking. "I see the bakery is closed, which is fine, because I can't make it to class today anyway. The biggest parade yet is tomorrow, and I'm debuting a new float."

"You're getting back on a float?"

She walked even faster, which was astonishing given the height of her pink stilettos.

"Yes."

"But last time—"

"Don't you remember what I said?" She stopped suddenly and met my gaze. The concealer underneath her eyes wasn't heavy enough to hide the dark circles. Her face was gaunt despite the blush and heavy eyeliner. "Butt out if you know what's good for you."

The numbers I'd just seen flashed in my head again. They were a warning. There was no mistake about that. And after what had happened at the Pelican Playhouse, I feared that another attempt would be made on Cindy's life.

But my gut told me she'd known that for a while.

"Just listen to me for a second," I insisted.

"I'm very busy right now. Perhaps we can talk after Mardi Gras, OK?" Her chest rose, showing off her plunging neckline as she breathed deep. She resumed her afternoon business, and my heart raced at the thought of another death in Misty Key.

"Ember!"

Stevie's voice pierced my ears.

The sound of tires skidding echoed all around me.

I looked back toward the bakery, horrified by what I was seeing.

The warning had been for someone else.

I'd crossed the street in a hurry, and I'd forgotten that a little black ball of fur followed me wherever I went.

Chapter 20

"I just heard the word *accident* and came right over."

Thad stood on my doorstep with a bundle of roses. I hesitated to reach for them, unsure if they were meant for me. A lump formed in my throat, and I swallowed hard. Thad leaned on the opposite foot, repositioning his stance and doing his best to make sure the flowers couldn't be seen from next door.

"Wait, who called you?"

"Aqua," he answered. "Didn't I mention that?"

"She did?" I muttered. "Of course she did."

"You don't look like you've been hit by a car." His eyes darted from my jeans to the T-shirt I'd borrowed from Aqua since all of my tops were in the wash. It was tighter than what I usually wore, but I'd figured it didn't matter since I was spending the evening at home.

"That's because I wasn't."

Thad slightly lowered the roses.

"I'm confused," he responded.

"Whiskers was hit by a car," I explained.

"Oh." The bundle of flowers rested gently at his side. He narrowed his eyes and avoided looking straight at me. "Now that you mention it, I do remember her saying something about a cat. And I guess it is strange that she told me to come to the house and not the hospital."

"Yeah." A subtle smile crossed my face. "But it's the thought that counts, right?"

"True." He handed me the flowers with a chuckle.

"Don't worry, I won't tell the clan."

"Tell them what?" He stepped inside, and I shut the front door.

"That you bought a bouquet of roses for a cat," I finished.

"They wouldn't be for a cat if I gave them to you though." He took a step closer so that the minty scent of breath was inches from me.

"No," I said quietly.

"Good. You came." Aqua popped into the living room, her purple-streaked hair up in a ponytail. I immediately took a step away from Thad and smelled the bouquet.

"Yeah, we need to talk," I said.

"I wanted Thad to come over, and now he's here." Aqua carried on the conversation as if it wasn't a big deal she'd called Thad and made him think I was injured.

"You better have a good reason." I held up the flowers. "Otherwise, you owe him."

"Aw, how sweet," Aqua cooed like the bundle of roses was a bundled newborn. "Now, follow me."

Aqua jogged upstairs and into her bedroom. Thad eyed me suspiciously. I shrugged. I didn't know what Aqua was up to or why she required Thad's assistance. I set the roses down on the coffee table and walked with him up the stairs.

Whiskers was lying in Aqua's bed with a bandaged paw. He was lucky to be alive, and after a stressful trip to the vet, it was clear that Whiskers's power, if he had one, was in no way related to healing or pain management.

"Aqua, what's this about?" I asked her.

"I helped a squirrel the other day," she replied.

"Good for you?" I tugged at the tight T-shirt that hugged my torso, curious what Thad thought of it.

"My point is that I communicated with him," Aqua went on. "For the record, all squirrels are insane. But then I thought if I was able to help a random critter in our yard, why can't I communicate with Whiskers?"

"Easy," I explained. "You're still growing and practicing your talent."

"Or what if Whiskers isn't an animal at all?" Aqua raised her eyebrows. "This is where Thad comes in. Thad, you're human."

"Last time I checked." He glanced down at his jeans.

"I can't hear your thoughts as a human, but what about when you're a wolf?" Aqua looked him up and down. "If you shif,t and I can't hear your thoughts when you're in canine form that makes sense, right? I mean, there's still a bit of human in you."

"So you want me to shift?" Thad observed her expression with caution. "Are you sure that's wise? I don't want to give the cat a heart attack."

"Please," Aqua pleaded. "Just do it, and let me try and communicate with you the way I do with Yogi.

You're the only person I know that I can test my theory on. Please. Please. Please."

"Are you OK with all of this?" Thad turned to me for permission.

"It can't hurt anything." I tucked a wavy strand of hair behind my ear and debated whether or not to close my eyes. The first time I'd seen Thad shift had been terrifying. His fangs were sharp, and there had been a wild spark in his eyes that reminded me of a ravenous beast. But it had been easier to watch each time he did it.

"OK, ladies. You asked for it."

Aqua stayed close to Whiskers as Thad's solid stature changed from man to wolf in the blink of an eye. One moment, he stood upright with dark hair, a sharp chin, and inviting hickory eyes. In one swift movement, he wasn't a man anymore.

Whiskers hissed and Aqua petted him as best she could to calm him down.

"Relax, Whiskers," Aqua said. "He's not here for an evening snack. I promise."

Whiskers squirmed, attempting to run away, but his paw stopped him from leaving the comforts of Aqua's cloudy blue comforter.

"Well?" I replied as Thad nudged my leg with the tip of his nose. His messy fur smelled like the swamps just outside of town. I pressed my lips together, wondering what he would say if I offered to give his canine half a good scrub.

"Give me a minute or two." When Aqua was satisfied that Whiskers wouldn't risk another injury to dart out of the room, she closed her eyes. She took a few breaths, holding out her hands like she was deep in meditation.

"Anything?"

"Hang on." Aqua opened her eyes and stared at Thad. She took some more deep breaths. After a few more minutes, she shook her head. "OK, you can shift back now."

A moment later, Thad was standing next to me in human form.

Whiskers got comfy again.

"So, did it work?" Thad raised his eyebrows. "I was thinking something very specific. Any idea what it was?"

"You're hungry for fried chicken and biscuits?" Aqua bit the side of her lip. Thad shook his head. "So, my hunch was right." She glanced back at Whiskers.

"What are you saying?" I asked.

"I'm saying I can't connect with Thad because he's not fully wolf," Aqua explained. "But I can connect with Yogi and other critters I come across because they're all animal. I'm not a mind reader. Of humans, I mean."

"So, you think Whiskers isn't..." It was an odd thought. One that creeped me out.

"Yeah." Aqua laughed, looking pleased with herself. "Whiskers isn't all cat. He can't be. Otherwise, I would've figured him out a long time ago."

The three of us studied Whiskers as he looked up at us. His big yellow eyes were wide and innocent, and his black coat was nestled snuggly into Aqua's comforter.

"So then what exactly are you?" I stared directly at Whiskers like I expected him to answer. He didn't. He didn't even meow.

"Wow." Thad nodded. "Nice work, Aqua."

"I guess the Grants really have been hiding something," I added. I wondered what it was; it could have been anything. Whiskers could have been cursed, he could have been a reincarnated family member, or he could be the result of a spell gone horribly wrong.

"If it'll get the Grants in trouble, Stevie will be happy." Aqua untied her mop of purplish hair and started forming it into a loose braid that fell past her shoulders.

"I'm impressed," I said. "You figured it out."

"I wish I could say the same about you," Aqua chided.

"OK, rude."

"I'm serious." Aqua gently patted Whiskers. "The police have shut down the bakery, and you're hanging around the house in my old T-shirt from summer camp."

I immediately turned away from Thad so he wouldn't give the shirt a second look.

"The bakery is closed?" Thad gently nudged my shoulder. "Why didn't you tell me?"

"If I were you, I would use my time off for good." Aqua cleared her throat. "All right. Now get out of my room."

Thad and I walked back downstairs and into the living room. I felt the heat of Thad's stare. I'd dragged him along for a ride, and I knew I owed some sort of explanation. I fixated on the roses.

"I'll just put these in water." I reached for the fragile bundle and headed for the kitchen but Thad softly grabbed my arm. My heart pounded.

"What's going on? You're not giving up, are you?"

"No," I responded, lowering my voice. "No. It's just...things keep getting even more complicated, and Stevie hates me, and the bakery is in trouble, and I still don't know if I should take that job in New York..." I stopped and took a deep breath. "Sometimes I just don't know where I fit, you know?"

"You're preaching to the choir." Thad grinned, and it made me feel a little less overwhelmed.

"No matter what I do to try and help, *something* goes wrong." My eyes wandered to the empty staircase. "What happened to Whiskers is a prime example."

"Well, for starters, we don't even know what Whiskers is. And second, you've got to stop letting Stevie get in your head. You are not to blame." Thad sat on the couch in the living room and waited for me to join him. I sat next to him, leaning back on a pillow and attempting to stop myself from blurting out all of my problems. Thad had a way of making me comfortable and *uncomfortable* at the same time. It must be the grin.

"And if I'm the murderer?" I teased.

"Then I blame you for everything."

"There's got to be a logical explanation for how that red velvet cheesecake ended up in Room 111," I continued, thinking back on the day I'd walked into the crime scene. "Someone must have seen something. Every single one of our students couldn't have taken their cheesecakes home and eaten them straight away. I wish I knew who was lying."

"What does your gut tell you?" Thad leaned forward and placed his elbows on his knees, studying me intensely.

"Rickiah wouldn't lie to me," I answered. "I actually saw Zinny's cheesecake so I know she was telling truth."

"And the others?"

"I can't be certain." I shook my head. I was left with four different possibilities. I couldn't imagine Darlene aiding in a crime even though, according to Stevie, one of her dead relatives claimed she was living in sin. Whatever that had meant. Cindy definitely didn't finish an entire red velvet cheesecake on her own. Kalen's secret was out in the open now, but that didn't mean he didn't have more, and Mary Jean had a dirty past she didn't want getting out.

"You must have a hunch," Thad commented.

"Yeah." I gulped. "A couple of things keep leading me back to the hotel. Kalen works there, so who knows what he might have seen?"

"Or done," Thad added.

"And then there's Mary Jean." I rubbed the side of my face. Reasoning with her had been next to impossible. "She's definitely hiding something."

"Mary Jean it is then." Thad clasped his hands together. "Where do we start?"

"*We?*"

"Yes, *we*," he replied. "Saving the bakery is in my best interest too."

"Yeah?" I smiled. "And why is that?"

"Because it's another reason for you to stay in Misty Key."

Chapter 21

I'd never hacked into a computer before.

Which was why Thad had come up with a plan to distract the receptionist while I searched for records relating to Room 111.

"I know for a fact that Mrs. Carmichael will be on everyone's case today making sure everything is perfect," Thad whispered. The two of us stood outside the main entrance of the Crystal Grande Hotel. To my surprise, the lobby was full of guests waiting for a table at the hotel restaurant.

"Doesn't she expect that every day?"

"Yes, but today is Fat Tuesday," Thad replied. "And the day is packed with one party after another."

"Apparently starting with brunch." I eyed the crowd of people outside the hotel restaurant. Most of them were dressed for summer weather with minimal attire. It wasn't quite as warm as a summer day, but the humidity was enough to stop a bikini-clad woman from freezing.

"Are you ready for this?" Thad glanced down at Yogi, and I clutched the strap of my purse.

"Now, don't get too excited. This is a one-time thing." I knelt next to Yogi and opened my bag. I pulled out a plastic container I'd used to mix a healthy amount of water and dirt from the backyard. The resulting goop was enough to make anyone run for help.

"Remember, find everything you can about Room 111, and I'll keep watch."

"How can you be sure the receptionist will leave her desk?" I asked, my heart racing as I visualized myself at the computer over and over again.

Thad paused and narrowed his eyes as he studied the smiling blonde—the first person a guest saw when entering the lobby.

"The power of suggestion." He nodded. "Don't worry. I'll get you a good five minutes."

"Only five?" My pulse quickened even more. I was great at controlling my nerves when it came to business presentations but sleuthing felt completely different. I never knew what was waiting for me around the next corner.

And I never knew if today was the day I would be caught.

"That's plenty of time for someone like you," Thad answered.

"You mean a numbers nerd?" I took a deep breath and dipped each of Yogi's paws into the thick mud in my container. When I'd made sure there was enough to leave footprints on the shiny lobby floor, I nudged Yogi inside. "Go on."

Yogi strolled in unnoticed at first. He sniffed the air, and then caught sight of a trash can near the restrooms. Yogi couldn't resist a fresh heap of garbage, especially if it contained dirty napkins, gum, and leftover room service.

A trail of mud followed Yogi everywhere he went. A couple of guests noticed and pointed, and then a few more. Finally, a woman stepping off of the elevator gasped, and the lobby broke out into hushed whispers.

"This is my cue." Thad cleared his throat before dashing into the hotel and stopping right in front of the woman at the front desk. He ran his hands through his hair and glared at Yogi.

"My supervisor will not be happy about this," he said in a panic. "Neither will *yours*."

The woman flapped her hands as she looked at the mud and then back at Thad.

"I...um..." The woman's eyes went wide as Yogi began licking a section of the wall.

I covered my mouth, holding back laughter. I never would have pegged Thad as an actor, but he had some skills.

"I'll handle the dog." Thad inched toward Yogi like he was a ferocious beast that needed taming. "You grab a maid. Quick!"

"Yes! Of course." The woman darted from her post and disappeared down the hall. She would be back any minute with someone to help clean the floors.

It's now or never.

I ran behind the front desk, and the first thing that caught my eye was a deck of face cards on the computer screen. The receptionist had been playing solitaire. A smirk crossed my face, and I focused on the scene behind it. It contained a window allowing the user to pull up reservations by date and by name. I searched the program for a field allowing me to type in a room number. My stomach leaped when I found it.

I typed in Room 111 and narrowed my search from the beginning of the year to the present. A list popped up onto the screen, and I quickly hit *print*. I tapped my foot as I glanced at over my shoulder at Thad. He'd grabbed Yogi's collar and was watching the hallway in front of him like a hawk. He ignored the dirty looks from onlookers and wrinkled his nose.

Thad's eyes locked with mine. I ducked, waiting for the list to finish printing.

"Mr. H." Thad's voice rang through the lobby like a clap of thunder. My chest went tight, and a bead of sweat formed on my brow as I stared at the printer. My list was almost done printing.

"Where did that dog come from?" The voice of the man I'd met on the beach, Mrs. Carmichael's new business partner, boomed like a ship crashing against the shoreline.

"Outside?" Thad replied.

"Well, get it out of here," Harrison muttered. "Take it to the pound. I really don't care. Just get it out."

"Yes, sir," Thad replied.

"And get back to your desk, Gracie," he instructed. "Sorry for the disturbance, folks. We've got it all under control." The tone of his voice changed when he addressed his guests. It was friendlier and more upbeat.

I breathed a sigh of relief when my list finished printing. I shoved it into my purse and proceeded to crawl back into the lobby. I was met by Gracie, the bouncy blonde who sat behind the desk. Her nude heels stopped directly in front of me, and I casually looked up.

"Can I help you, miss?" Her eyes darted to her boss, Mr. H.

"I, um, dropped an earring," I lied, continuing to crawl past her. "I think it rolled back here somewhere."

"Oh." Gracie's stunned expression immediately changed. She knelt down and scanned the floor. "Let me help you."

"That's OK." I forced a friendly giggle. "You know, it wasn't that expensive. I'll just buy a new one."

"Maybe my boss can—"

"No." My stomach churned at the thought of having to explain myself to Mr. H, and by extension, Mrs. Carmichael. "No. That's OK."

"Oh, there you are." Thad cleared his throat, his eyes wider than clementines as he stared at me.

"You know each other?" Gracie narrowed her eyes.

"Yes." Thad grabbed my hand and helped me up. Yogi sat lazily at his side.

"How?" Gracie took her spot behind the counter, and I studied Harrison as he shook hands with guests and rolled his eyes when a maid arrived one second too late. So far, he hadn't spotted me.

"We're...uh..." My eyes stayed locked on Harrison.

"Siblings," I blurted out.

"Dating," Thad said at the same time.

Gracie twirled a strand of her long blonde hair and eyed us both suspiciously. Her hand reached for her mouse, and she slowly dragged her attention back to her computer.

"Y'all are too strange for me," she commented. "Which is it? Are you related or are you dating? Please don't tell me it's both."

"Heavens, no," I answered. "We're...um...the dating thing. That's what I meant."

"Yep," Thad agreed.

Harrison observed the maid as she cleaned the floor one muddy paw print at a time. When he was satisfied, he turned to leave. But his eye caught sight of Yogi first. I whipped around to stop him from noticing me, and I came face to face with Thad's chest.

He leaned down, his thick hands caressing my cheek.

And then he did something I wasn't expecting. Thad kissed me.

"Get that mutt out of here or you're fired!"

Thad pulled away, holding my shoulders steady as Harrison yelled at the back of my head.

"You got it, sir," he replied.

"Aw, you two are sweet," Gracie cooed, sitting down at her desk and returning to her game of solitaire. "How long have y'all been together?"

"About five seconds," I muttered.

Chapter 22

"Hands off the buns!"

Stevie's baking obsession had spilled into the house. The kitchen table was full of baked goods. Everything from cupcakes to pound cakes covered every surface. The counter was full of ingredients, and the constant use of the oven had heated the entire main level. I fanned my face with a scrap of paper as Stevie shooed Orion from a pan of hot pecan sticky buns.

"I promise I'll eat all my dinner, Ma."

"I've heard that one before," Stevie stated. "So, are you going to tell me what you found? Aqua overheard your little plan."

"Yeah." I'd been in a daze since the moment I'd walked through the door. Thad had stayed behind at the hotel for his shift, and I'd raced home with Yogi. "I looked up Room 111, and apparently Mary Jean has booked it three times in the past week."

"That little liar," Stevie murmured. "She probably did it. She probably killed George and is about to get away with it."

"Murdered with poison. The killer has to be a lady." Orion smirked and discreetly touched another sticky bun when his mother's back was turned.

"What makes you such an expert?" Aqua stared at her phone as he walked to the fridge and pulled out a pitcher of sweet tea.

"TV," he answered. "Don't you watch TV?"

"Probably not as much as you do," Stevie replied. "Hands off! What did I just say?"

Orion rolled his eyes and took a few steps back, although I was pretty sure he planned on grabbing one at an opportune moment and then running for his life. It was hard to resist Stevie's baking. She had a true talent for it, and I was slowly starting to understand why she felt so lost without the bakery.

But the bakery wasn't doomed yet.

"Last time we talked to her, it didn't go so well," I went on.

Stevie continued organizing her baked desserts and lining up ingredients for one of her well-known recipes—red Bama cookies, a red velvet cookie with white chocolate chunks. She hadn't looked me directly in the eye for more than a second since Sunday.

"But now we have evidence," Stevie said. "She can't deny that she booked the room where George was killed. I'm sure the police have already talked to her about it too. She has to know that something like that won't stay secret for long."

"So, what do you propose?"

"I finish these Bama cookies, have my dinner, and watch the parade," Stevie responded.

"You even the least bit curious, Stevie?" Aqua poured a bunch of sweet tea into the tallest glass she could find. "That's not like you at all."

"My hands are tied on this one." Stevie didn't bother looking at Aqua when she said it. The bakery hadn't officially closed, although we had no idea when it would be officially open again. But Stevie was already a baker without a bakery—an artisan without a purpose.

"Why not just march up to her and demand the truth?" Aqua shrugged as if getting a straight answer out of Mary Jean was a piece of cake. "Three guesses where she is right now."

"If she admits to the police that she took the red velvet cheesecake to the murder scene, then that could put us in the clear." I threw the thought out there. It was true. But admitting to that would also be like admitting to murder, and no one in their right mind would do that, especially not a God-fearing woman like Mary Jean.

Stevie stopped what she was doing and sighed.

"I hate it when you're right," she muttered. "If the police haven't figured out by now that we're not to blame, I don't know if they ever will."

"What do you say we rock Mary Jean's world one last time?" A flutter of excitement engulfed my stomach. We were close to the truth. I knew Stevie felt it too. At the forefront of my mind was the ghost of George Carmichael and all of the things he'd told us. At the back of my mind was Thad.

"Count me out," Aqua said. "Whiskers has been whining all day. I've also committed to watching him day and night to see if he's a secret shifter or something."

"He could be a weird old guy," Orion suggested.

"I'm rooting for a hot *young* guy," Aqua said. "Whatever he is, I'm so close to figuring it out."

"And I'm sure that's what the Grants are afraid of," I commented. "But one problem at a time."

"Why do I feel like I'm miles behind you two?" Stevie glared at Aqua.

"I'll tell you about it later." Aqua took a sip of her sweet tea. "I've got to get back to the little critter. We're halfway through season three of *Passions of the South*. Maribelle just found out that her brother is the father of the mayor's wife's love child. He's pretty into it."

"Oh, is that the episode where Maribelle's uncle climbs through the bathroom window and falls into the bathtub?" Orion perked up.

"While Sue Ellen was having a bubble bath," Aqua finished. She laughed. "Yep. Classic Elmer and Sue Ellen."

"When did you watch that?" Stevie scolded him.

"Um..." Orion grinned, his eyes round like a puppy dog's. "I'm ready for those vegetables now."

"Go check on your grandma." Stevie dismissed him with a wave. "She's in her room reading."

"OK." He skipped out of the kitchen, and I guessed that he was glad to.

"I have a bad feeling about all of this," Stevie said slowly when it was just the three of us and Yogi. "Have you seen Main Street today? It's more crowded than that pan of sticky buns."

"The parade is what worries me," I added. My blood ran cold as I remembered the moment I'd heard an explosion outside the Pelican Playhouse. "What if there's another explosion? I don't know. Some things add up, and some don't."

"I guess we better get changed." Stevie wiped her hands on her T-shirt and glanced down at her jean shorts.

"Changed?" I didn't plan on switching my casual outfit for a skirt and heels.

"It's Mardi Gras, Ember. We gotta blend in."

* * *

The sun was setting as jazz music echoed up and down Main Street. The sidewalks were crowded, and tourists wandered from shop to shop and back up the hill to the Crystal Grande Hotel. I saw everything from screaming toddlers in bead-covered strollers to college drinkers to tourists who looked to be older than my granny. Fat Tuesday drew the attention of just about everyone in Alabama, and celebrations were in full swing.

I hadn't made the mistake of wearing a dress this time. I'd chosen black slacks and a sleeveless blouse that would soon be doused with glittery beads. Stevie wore a tube top and jeans that were sure to make her stick out like a carrot in a donut box once we got to the hotel. But her top would definitely garner Mary Jean's disapproval, which was what she might've been thinking when she'd raided her closet.

Yogi had tagged along too. He already had a sparkly purple string of beads around his neck. He looked more festive than I did.

"I don't see any signs, do you?" I searched the crowd as we walked toward the hotel. I'd expected to see Mary Jean and her posse in the middle of the action. She never missed an opportunity to point out the sinners. "Maybe she decided to back off tonight?"

"Are you kidding?" Stevie shook her head and pulled at the neckline of her tube top. "Mardi Gras without Bible quotes and repentance pamphlets is like eating a cupcake without the frosting. Who would do that? They go hand in hand."

"People like muffins," I pointed out. "I eat muffins all the time."

"Muffins are different, Ember. They're not the same consistency as cake."

"Over there." I pointed ahead of me where a sign that said *Bead-ware of the Devil* pushed through the street.

I braced myself for the look on Mary Jean's face when she saw us again, but my eyes met someone else. I frowned. Stevie took a deep breath and began fanning her face. She glared from person to person, and sometimes she glared at empty gaps in between groups.

"Man, it's crowded." She touched her ear. "I haven't heard this much chatter since that guy passed out on stage at the bluegrass festival ten years ago."

"Is this chatter human?" I reached down and patted Yogi. "I mean *living* humans?"

"Excuse me." Stevie pulled aside the man with the sign. He immediately handed her a pamphlet. "I'm looking for Mary Jean?"

"Oh, she wasn't able to make it tonight," the man responded. "Sour stomach. It's too bad because there are lots of folks out here tonight who could use a good sermon about—"

"Yeah, yeah." Stevie nodded impatiently. "I know all about that, Norm. I live here."

"Oh." He squinted and gave Stevie a second look. "I thought you had a familiar face. Will we see you at church on Sunday?"

Yogi barked as if answering for her.

Religion was a soft spot for most psychics, Stevie especially.

Norm jumped and looked down at Yogi before continuing to work the crowd.

Stevie frowned at me. "I guess she's too ashamed to show her face?"

"Or something's wrong?" I shook my head. "We need to find her. I've got her address in my office."

Stevie was no longer paying any attention to me at all. Her focus had settled down the street. She stood frozen, and I followed her gaze. I was met with a handsy couple headed to the seafood place near the marina and a stumbling group of women chanting their college fight song.

Stevie hadn't been watching either of them.

"She's pissed," Stevie muttered. "Bless her little dead heart. She had lost her mind."

"Who?"

"That woman I saw at Darlene's," she answered.

"The dead relative who is convinced that her great-granddaughter is Lucifer's offspring?" I glanced down the street at Darlene's antiques shop. At first glance, it looked closed, but then I spotted a faint light shining through one of the display windows.

"That's the one." Stevie continued to watch a section of sidewalk near the antiques shop. "She's letting the world know what she thinks about Mardi Gras, even though the world can't hear her. She's stuck on a loop about the unholy state of Misty Key and poor Darlene."

"Sounds exhausting," I commented.

"Shooting stars, she sees me." Stevie cleared her throat and averted her gaze. She turned her head and stood silent for a moment.

"Is she giving you a talking to?"

Stevie nodded in response, and Yogi barked.

I clasped my hands together and avoided any sort of physical contact. I'd reached my ghost-seeing limit for the year. If I saw any more spirits yelling at me, I would need a whole lot of medication to get to sleep every night. There was only so much meditation and whale sounds could do.

"Let's go." Stevie crossed the street, and I followed, keeping my eyes on Yogi the entire time. Stevie marched right up to Darlene's shop and peeked through the windows. She knocked on the front door, ignoring the *Closed* sign displayed on the other side of the glass. No one answered.

Stevie jiggled the handle.

"You're just going to walk right in?" I whispered.

"Why not?" Stevie glanced back at the street as tourists rushed back and forth, too consumed in their own conversations to notice what was going on around them.

"What if Darlene's *sins* consist of in-store naughtiness with her husband? Do you really want to walk in on that?" I wrinkled my nose at the thought.

"If that's what's upsetting her great-grandmother, then good for her," Stevie replied. "Also, I'm pretty sure she would have locked the door."

"Maybe chancing it is part of the thrill?"

"Are you speaking from experience here?" Stevie paused and looked me up and down.

"No," I blurted out.

"Then stop blushing."

I touched my cheek. It didn't feel hot at all, but by the time I'd formed a comeback in my head, Stevie was already inside. I stepped into Darlene's store, unsure if calling her name was the best thing to do. Yogi trotted quietly behind and began his usual sniffing.

The sound of laughter made me stop in my tracks. Most of Darlene's antiques were just as she'd left them last time we'd visited her. The vintage olive-colored fridge was still for sale by the register, and a shelf of porcelain dolls hanging on the opposite wall was enough to make my skin crawl. A glow came from the hallway leading to the back of the store, and Stevie didn't hesitate to follow it.

I balled my hands into fists as I walked faster and hit the back of Stevie's head with my nose when she stopped suddenly. Yogi's paw hit my heels. More light illuminated the storage room behind Darlene's office. I was surprised to see smiling faces, a cart of booze, and a circular table at the center of the room.

"It's about time." Darlene wore a clear green sun visor and a T-shirt that said *What Happens in Vegas*. Her eyes were fixated on a deck of cards. "We were beginning to think you weren't going to..." She finally looked up, and her eyes widened when she saw Stevie and me—our mouths hanging open.

"You're not Roberta," a woman sitting next to her with a matching visor exclaimed. "Roberta was supposed to bring the sorghum cookies. You promised me sorghum cookies tonight, Darlene."

"Don't get your panties in a twist, Joni."

The group of women laughed.

"Darlene," Stevie gasped. Darlene clutched her cards and hobbled over to meet us.

"I knew I should've locked the door and let Roberta call me when she got here," Darlene muttered. "Please don't say anything about this. The Misty Key Women's Society doesn't approve, and they'd kick us all out if they knew."

"I'll keep my mouth shut on one condition." Stevie's glare was enough to melt the red and black poker chips on the table. "Y'all *have* to invite me next time."

Yogi poked his head out from behind my legs, his tail wagging excitedly at the prospect of making new friends who might toss him a few scraps.

"It seems that everyone is welcome." I nudged Stevie. A woman at the table had been hiding her face, but I knew who she was. I bit the side of my lip and waited for Stevie to get up to speed.

"Oh, you've got to be kidding." Stevie didn't bother lowering her voice. "We need to talk, M.J."

Sitting next to a very disappointed Joni was Mary Jean.

And with her green visor on, she didn't look the least bit innocent.

Chapter 23

"So, I have a problem." Mary Jean held up her hands and dropped them to her sides.

"No, no." Stevie folded her arms. "My ten-year-old has problems. You have a disease or something."

The three of us stood in the darkened antiques shop with Yogi standing guard near the front entrance. Darlene had continued with her game of poker after giving us an explanation about the underground gambling ring, consisting of countless Misty Key residents; she'd been running it for the past five years.

"You don't understand," Mary Jean muttered. "I don't have a choice, OK. I *need* the money."

"We all need money, Mary Jean." Stevie shook her head. "We're all human. Most of us. And you'll get nowhere in life if you keep pointing the finger of blame at other people." Stevie paused, taking a deep breath and looking right at me. She hung her head as she collected her thoughts.

"I'm about to lose my house." Mary Jean lowered her head in defeat. "I don't understand. I've prayed for help my entire life, and now when I need it the most, I'm about to be tossed out on the streets."

"Have you tried asking other people for help, not just praying for it?" Stevie tilted her head as if the Bible was common knowledge. "You help others, and then you let others help *you*. That's how it works, M.J."

"I won two hundred dollars my first time playing with the ladies," Mary Jean explained. "I used the money to sign up for your class. I thought the extra skills would come in handy. It appears that beginner's luck really is a thing because I'm down one hundred bucks tonight."

"I'll give you a ten if you tell us the truth about Room 111," I said.

Mary Jean's lip curled.

"I'm not a tramp." She sighed. "And if I would have known that Mr. Carmichael was going to be..." She scratched the side of her shoulder. "Put it this way. I regret doing it, but I was desperate."

"Doing what?" Stevie tapped her foot, trying to be patient.

"I was hired to book that room using my name," she confessed. "I did it for the extra cash. I didn't think anything of it until Mr. Carmichael died."

"Who hired you?"

Mary Jean shrugged. "I don't know. I got an anonymous text from someone who knew I needed money. Once they explained the job, I did it. It was easy. Book the room at the hotel, and then I got paid."

"The Peppers are looking for some weekend help at the marina," Stevie said. "I'll give them your name, OK?"

Mary Jean nodded and patted her eye. It appeared to be nothing in the dim light of the antiques shop, but instinct told me she was holding back a tear or two. Whatever had driven Mary Jean to lead a double life couldn't have been easy to live with. If anything, her confession, even if it was just to us, had lightened her burdens.

"Thank you." Mary Jean forced a smile as her eyes darted to Stevie's tube top.

"Not a word." Stevie pointed her finger at her.

"Yes, I get it." Mary Jean exhaled loudly. "May I offer you a jacket?"

"That's better." Stevie covered as much skin as she could with her arms. "Thanks for not calling me a heathen or a whore."

"Yes, well I should get back to my game. Maybe I'll get my money back."

As Mary Jean rejoined the group, Stevie glanced down at her tube top.

"I don't look like I'm trying to be sixteen again, do I?"

"I don't think you would have worn that as a sixteen-year-old," I commented. "You wouldn't have been able to hold it up."

"I was a late bloomer." She placed her hands on her hips. The two of us laughed. "Listen, Ember, that whole finger-of-blame stuff—"

"You don't have to say anything," I interrupted.

"I do." Stevie took a deep breath as the sound of more laughter trickled in from the back room. "I've been out of my mind with worry since the second Detective Winter came knocking. I know it's not your fault one of our cakes ended up at the Crystal Grande. I'm still trying to process all of this."

"The bakery is your baby," I replied. "I never meant to put it in harm's way. And whatever you might think of me, the bakery is near and dear to my heart too. Dad left some pretty big shoes to fill, and I wonder every day if I'm screwing up his legacy."

"You're not." Stevie touched my arm. "You're making it better. The changes you've made needed to happen. I've just been too stubborn to admit I can't do everything."

"You don't have to." I wrapped my arms around her shoulders. My mind lingered on all the adventures I'd had since moving back to my hometown. I knew in my heart that I couldn't leave. The lives of my family members were too precious, and time went by too fast.

And then there was Thad.

"That's another mystery solved," Stevie said as she pulled away. "On to the next."

She scratched Yogi's ears.

My cell phone buzzed in my pocket, and I stared at the screen before answering it.

It was Thad.

Talking to Thad in front of Stevie would give everything away. She already studied me suspiciously for waiting until the third ring to even think about answering it. I cleared my throat and held the phone to my ear.

"Hi."

I expected a *hello* in response—an *I miss you* or a *where are you* or something along those lines.

"Get to the hotel as soon as you can," Thad responded.

"Um..." I touched my cheek. I was definitely blushing this time. "If this is about that thing that happened earlier, we agreed it was just for show."

"I'm not calling about that," he said.

Something in my heart wilted.

"You're not?"

"No. I mean, yes...I mean, just get over here. It's urgent." He stumbled over his words in a way I'd never heard him do before.

"Did the restaurant run out of gumbo?" I joked.

"No. Some woman is on the roof, and she's about to jump."

* * *

"For once, I'm glad you're here." Detective Winter spotted me in the lobby before I had the chance to talk to Thad. Yogi growled when the detective touched my shoulder. He swiftly retracted his hand.

"Nice to see you too, Detective."

A group of police officers stood behind him. I couldn't tell if they were waiting for the detective's next instructions or if they had been tasked with monitoring the party that spilled out of the ballroom and into every other crevice of the main level. With live music blaring and more crowds of people loitering in the lobby and waiting for the night parade to begin, I could hardly hear my own voice.

"I need you to come with me to the fourth floor," he said.

"I'm coming too," Stevie insisted.

"The dog isn't allowed upstairs," he said.

"He can stay with me." Thad stood next to me and reached for Yogi's collar. He nodded at Stevie and me.

"Right this way," the detective said.

Detective Winter led us to an elevator separated from the ones used by guests. It was the private elevator that led to the Carmichael suites. A code was needed to ride it to the top floor. I'd ridden in it once with Luann, and once had been enough. Stevie and I stepped inside with the detective and a couple of police officers.

The elevator dinged as we reached the top floor, and the door opened to a long hallway with more police officers. Mrs. Carmichael and her business partner, Harrison, stood outside her son, Jonathon's, room. It was across the hall from George's old suite where he'd hidden from the world for years. I glanced up and down the hall, wondering how many more secret rooms and tunnels were hidden behind the walls. Since George had designed the top floor, anything was possible.

"Right this way. She has been asking for you." The detective escorted us into the sitting area of Jonathon Carmichael's room, where the patio doors were open and more officers stood on the balcony looking up.

"Who?"

"She says she knows you," the detective explained. "Her name is Cindy Buford."

Stevie and I exchanged nervous glances.

"She's a student of mine," Stevie responded.

"She asked for Ember," the detective clarified. He gestured toward the balcony. "Just talk to her and see if you can convince her to come down."

"And if she jumps?" I gulped. I didn't want to be responsible for something so horrible.

"Stay calm, and take it one step at a time," he instructed. "My instincts tell me she just needs to talk."

"This is a weird way of doing it," Stevie muttered.

The night air brushed across my face as I stepped onto the balcony with the sounds of guests below me. Some were laughing on the beach, some were trying to get a better look at Cindy, and some just wanted to watch for the thrill of it. An officer held a ladder leading up to the roof and assisted me with the first few steps.

"I'm *really* glad I didn't wear a dress," I said.

The ladder wobbled a little as I climbed higher. My chest went tight, and I forced myself to look straight ahead rather than looking down. My stomach churned regardless, and my extremities felt tingly, as though the higher altitude was making me light-headed.

"He did find you." Cindy sniffled, wiping away tears as she sat facing the ocean. Her green party dress flowed in the evening breeze, her blonde curls covered part of her face, and black streaks of makeup ringed her eyes.

"Cindy." My heart jumped as I moved carefully from shingle to shingle to join her.

Don't look down. Don't slip. And, don't look down.

"I'm sorry to throw you in the middle of everything like this." She sniffled again. "You were right. You were right all along."

"Cindy, can't we have this conversation somewhere else?" My heart beat so loud I could hear it. I placed a hand on my chest, but that wasn't enough to calm myself down. My brain couldn't let go of the fear brewing in the pit of my stomach—the fear that I could fall to my death if I wasn't careful.

"I can't go back in there," Cindy replied. "Someone is trying to kill me."

"Jumping off the roof isn't the answer."

"I'm not going to jump, Ember." She brushed a strand of hair from her face. "Gosh, I must look awful right now."

"Then why did you tell the police you're going to jump?"

"So they would take me seriously and go find you," she answered.

"What happened, Cindy?"

"It's all a blur." She attempted to clean up the smudges around her eyes. "You're the only one who can help me."

"OK. What can I do?" I reached for her hand, hoping she would take it and make the journey back down the ladder and to the balcony.

"I don't know." She sighed and stared at the sea. The moon's reflection glowed in each wave.

"Did you climb up here all by yourself?"

"Acrobatics." Cindy nodded, and some of the sadness left her eyes.

"Listen." My heart was still beating out of control. "Come back inside, and let me help you explain everything to the police. If anyone can figure out who's trying to kill you, it's them. And don't quote me on this, but Detective Winter isn't half bad."

"So, he isn't a heartless prick like everyone says?"

"I said not to quote me."

"All right." A half-smile crossed her face. "But promise me you'll hold my hand. OK?"

"Sure."

"Swear it," she insisted.

"OK, I swear."

My legs were stiffer than week-old baguettes as I carefully walked back to the ladder. Cindy followed and waited until I stood firmly on the balcony before she began her descent. I held out my hand at her insistence, and she grabbed it the moment her foot touched the ground.

"Cindy Buford, I'm placing you under arrest for the murder of George Carmichael—"

"No!" Cindy shouted as Detective Winter moved toward her.

"Wait a second!" I held out my hand to try and stop him. "You never told me you were going to arrest her."

In one swift movement, Cindy pulled a knife from the bust of her dress and wrapped an arm around my chest. I felt pressure on my throat as the cold blade touched my skin, pressing just enough I felt the color drain from my face.

"No one move or she dies!" Cindy yelled, and her muscles tensed, drawing me in tighter.

She'd tricked me—used me as a pawn in whatever game she'd been playing with the police.

"Cindy," I whispered.

"Just shut up if you know what's good for you," she muttered in my ear.

One-by-one, each officer backed away as Cindy walked toward the exit, using me as a human shield. Stevie's eyes were wide with horror, and Detective Winter held up his hands with caution. His expression hadn't changed, and it was a relief to see that at least one person in the room wasn't panicking.

Mrs. Carmichael glared at Cindy as she pulled me into the hall and demanded that Mrs. Carmichael open the door to her suite. She did so with great disdain on her face, and Harrison squeezed her shoulder as Cindy forced me into the suite and locked the door behind us.

The minute we were alone, she loosened her grip and let me go.

Her chest heaved as she tried to catch her breath.

"Really, Cindy?" I touched the deadbolt on the door, but she pointed her knife right at me.

"Don't!" She clenched her jaw and took a deep breath. "Please, just give me a minute to think."

"You never told me you were wanted for murder," I responded.

"Would you have helped me if I had?" She held the knife steady, and I took a few steps away from the door.

"Maybe."

"I couldn't take that chance," she breathed. "Please, just give me a few minutes. Then you can open the door and leave."

I nodded, and she slowly lowered the knife, watching my hands. After a few seconds, she darted to the bedroom and opened Mrs. Carmichael's closet. My encounter with George's ghost came flooding back, and I couldn't help but laugh as I watched her run her hand along the wall and open the secret door leading to her escape.

"It's you," I said before she had the chance to disappear behind the wall. "You're the mistress. Of course you're the mistress. It all makes sense now."

The sound of banging rang through the room. The police were attempting to break down the door.

"Mistress?" She blinked repeatedly as she brushed more hair from her face.

"George's mistress," I added.

"How do you know that?" Her chest heaved even more when another loud bang blasted through the bedroom. She only had minutes left.

"That tunnel you're about to step into leads to Room 111. Cindy, be honest with me for once. What happened?"

"OK, yes. I loved George Carmichael more than anyone." She stared at the bedroom as if reminiscing about her lost love.

"It was your red velvet cheesecake that they found," I stated.

"I took him my latest creations after every class," she admitted. "Room 111 was our usual spot. We met there a few times a week."

"You hired Mary Jean to book the rooms," I added.

"I couldn't have my own name all over the books," she argued. "That would give me away. Besides, I heard from Darlene that Mary Jean was about to lose her house. I did her a favor."

"So, if you didn't kill George, who did?" I asked.

Another bang made Cindy panic. She put one foot inside the secret passageway, ready to disappear at any time.

"I don't know," she shouted back. "I came in our secret way so that no one would see me, and he was on the bed." A tear trickled down her face. "I didn't know what to do. The police would have blamed me for sure—the vengeful mistress. I was halfway home before I even remembered the cheesecake."

"You didn't pull it out of the box and cut a slice?"

"Heavens, no," she gasped. "There was no time for that."

"Did you see anything else? *Anyone* else?"

"No," she replied. "That night was just like every other. He went into the room first, had his coffee, and waited for me to come through the door in the closet."

The door to the suite burst open.

In an instant, Cindy had shut the closet door and disappeared.

"Are you OK?" Stevie immediately examined my neck.

"Yeah. I'm fine."

Stevie followed my gaze to the closet.

"Did she?"

"Oh, yeah," I muttered.

Detective Winter and his men searched the suite from top to bottom.

"It was Cindy?" Stevie shook her head, her midnight locks whipping from side to side. "Wow."

"She claims he was already dead when she entered the room," I muttered as a group of policemen ran back into the hallway.

"Do you believe her?"

"She could have been framed," I responded. "I mean she admitted to everything else. Her story lined up with George's."

"I want to talk to her." Stevie grabbed my wrist. I knew where she was taking me—the spot outside where Cindy would be exiting the secret passageway. She might already be outside.

The two of us ran out of the room and straight to the elevator. Mrs. Carmichael and Harrison were nowhere in sight. I anxiously waited for the *ding* and bit my lip as we waited for the elevator to take us down to the first floor.

Stevie and I ran, pushing through clusters of guests. Yogi barked in the background. He'd spotted us and was right on my heel. Thad would be right behind him. Stevie and I stumbled into the nighttime humidity, running along the side of the hotel that faced the beach.

I scanned my surroundings for any sign of Cindy. Unless she'd picked up some sort of disguise, she wouldn't be hard to miss with her brightly colored party dress and long blonde hair. My lungs burned, but I kept on sprinting. I'd been sitting at a desk for far too long.

Stevie stopped in front of me.

We were too late.

Yogi came to a halt at my side, and Thad touched the small of my back as he stopped right behind me.

Mrs. Carmichael stood with a group of police officers, her arms folded and a giant smirk across her petite face. Cindy was already in handcuffs, and tears streamed down her face as she yelled that she was innocent. The look in her eyes brought on memories of my mother's eyes at my father's funeral—empty and defeated.

"I know everything there is to know about this hotel," Mrs. Carmichael stated with her head held high. "That includes all of my husband's silly little passageways."

"I *didn't* kill him!" Cindy insisted.

"No you just slept with him and brought along a poisoned dessert that would do the trick," she replied. "I knew George had a mistress, but I can't believe it's been you all along, Cindy. I invited you to my ladies' luncheon last month, despite all of the rumors going around town about you. I even refer all of my guests to your theatre."

"This is all a mistake," Cindy insisted. "I did nothing wrong."

"Sleeping with my husband wasn't wrong?" Mrs. Carmichael's eyes went glossy.

"It's not illegal, Elizabeth."

Mrs. Carmichael turned her head.

"Get her out of here," she said.

Cindy shouted a few obscenities as the police pulled her to the nearest squad car.

"Is she really the killer?" Thad whispered in my ear.

"That depends." My stomach continued churning, and my heart went on racing as I watched Cindy duck her head and slip into the backseat. "She could be telling the truth, but she could also be lying."

"If only there was a way to sniff out the liars, huh, Thad?" Stevie joined the conversation with a slight grin. Cindy's arrest meant that the bakery had to be in the clear.

"No need for that," Thad answered. "The eyes usually give it away."

Chapter 24

Fat Tuesday had ended with a *bang*.

The good kind.

The night parade had gone as scheduled even though Cindy hadn't been present to dance on her new float. My mom hadn't minded, and Stevie had absorbed herself in enjoying the end-of-parade fireworks with Orion. Whether or not Cindy was guilty of murder, we all knew the bakery would be up and running again soon.

That realization had made Stevie smile the rest of the night.

"I don't know what to make first." Stevie ran her fingers along the counter. We'd gone in to work the next morning even though the bakery was still closed. Stevie was convinced that we would get a call from Detective Winter at any moment telling us our tests came back clear and we were allowed to open for business.

"Relax and enjoy the break," I responded. "He might not even call today. Sometimes it takes them forever to run those tests, and they took just about every pot, pan, and ingredient we had. I bet he'll call next week."

"Not if Cindy confesses," Stevie pointed out.

"I don't know."

"You still think she's innocent?" Stevie touched the side of her chin and watched me as I shrugged. The truth was I didn't know what to think.

"Generally speaking, definitely not. But is she a murderer?" I tilted my head. "I guess that depends on her relationship with George. We might never know that."

"Did you see Mrs. Carmichael?" Stevie chuckled. "Just when you think that family can't get any more dysfunctional."

"She didn't look too surprised, I'll give you that," I said. "I wonder if Cindy was George's first offense."

"Doubt it." Stevie shook her head and glanced at the door leading into the café. "Did you hear that?"

She walked quietly into the front of the bakery just as a soft knock rang through the room. Stevie unlocked the front door, surprised when she saw Mary Jean standing on the doorstep. She smiled, wearing a large T-shirt that covered most of her and loose-fitting jeans.

"Good, you're in." Mary Jean paused to catch her breath.

"Did you run all the way here or something?" Stevie narrowed her eyes.

"You two have no idea the kind of day I've had," Mary Jean replied, stepping into the empty bakery. "Ever since I told y'all the truth last night, I've been floating around on a cloud. I know the Lord will take care of me. I'm not worried about my house anymore."

"All that from a small confession?" Stevie crossed her arms, looking a bit skeptical as she soaked in Mary Jean's elated demeanor. I'd never seen her so happy.

"There's something I didn't tell you last night," Mary Jean continued. "In the spirit of confession, I wanted to lay *all* of my cards on the table, so here goes."

"You know we're not priests or pastors or whoever it is you're supposed to confess to, right?" Stevie wrinkled her nose.

"It doesn't matter." Mary Jean emitted another wide smile that changed the shape of her face. Her new persona was much more pleasant to be around. I covered my mouth as Stevie made a face as if she'd tasted something sour. "Am I going to need something strong after this? M.J., I don't even have sweet tea on hand."

"I was hired to lead those protests at the hotel," Mary Jean blurted out. Her words were followed by a loud exhale. "Oooh, that feels good to get off my chest."

"Who hired you?" I asked. "And why would someone do that? I don't get it."

"Don't know." She shook her head and held her hands up. "But I'm free. I'm free! Man, this feels great. You have no idea."

"How do you not know?" Stevie asked.

"Look, I thought it was God's wish," she explained. "The money showed up on my doorstep with the promise of more if I lead those protests."

My heart pounded.

"Were you told to protest the night George Carmichael was killed?"

Mary Jean nodded.

"*Crap.*"

"What is it?" Stevie focused on me, observing me from head to toe the same way she'd done to Mary Jean.

"There *was* a cover-up," I explained. "The protestors were a distraction. They pulled everyone's attention away from Room 111."

"Cindy could have hired her to do that too," Stevie pointed out. "I mean, she confessed to hiring Mary Jean to book that room."

"It was Cindy this whole time?" Mary Jean gasped. "Why would Cindy do that? She knew about the secret passageway. She could go in and out of that room undetected whenever she wanted."

"Then who hired you, Mary Jean?" Stevie asked.

"Probably the same person responsible for poisoning George's coffee and then staging the crime scene so that Cindy would take the fall." My heart raced, and there was no hope of calming down. The clues were finally adding up, and for once the riddle was clear.

George had been murdered, and the killer had set a trap for Cindy.

The question was who wanted George Carmichael dead?

"You think there's another mistress?" Stevie lowered her voice. She felt it in her gut too.

Cindy wasn't the killer.

The killer was still wandering around Misty Key.

* * *

"Who is in charge of room service?"

Kalen's eyes went wide as I questioned him for more information about the coffee that had been delivered to Room 111.

"This area is for employees only," Kalen answered. "You two aren't even supposed to be in here." Yogi growled. "No dogs allowed either."

"Just tell us, you little—"

"Stevie." I brushed her hands away from Kalen's collar. "Relax. He'll tell us."

"What's wrong with you two?" Kalen muttered, pushing his thick glasses up the bridge of his nose. "I need to change for my shift."

"It would be a shame if word about your little side hustle made its way to Detective Winter." Stevie had no problem threatening him. I knew her bark was worse than her bite. But Kalen didn't know that. "Now, tell us who is in charge of delivering food to Room 111."

"I don't know that sort of stuff, OK?" Kalen took a step back and smoothed his shirt. "You'll have to ask Mr. H. He's in charge of the scheduling, and it changes every day."

"You better hope he's in there," Stevie added.

"Whatever, Stevie."

"She means *thank you* for the information," I said.

Stevie and I headed to the manager's office where Harrison had set up shop. Yogi trailed behind us, stopping to sniff every cleaning cart and laundry bag we passed on the way. Stevie pointed to an office at the end of the hall. She'd been there before with Junior and Rickiah. I was confident she would be able to break in again if it came to that.

I tried the door, and it swung open.

The office was empty.

"Schedules," Stevie whispered, thumbing through papers on the desk. "If I were a schedule, where would I be?"

"The computer?" I suggested. I moved the mouse and stared at the computer screen. A log-in page popped up. "Any password ideas in that brain of yours?"

"Not one." Stevie moved on to the filing cabinets.

My eyes darted around the office for anything personal that might help. I froze when my eyes passed over something that might have changed the murder investigation from day one. But I hadn't ventured through Harrison's office before. Stevie and the others had.

Not me.

"No way," I said under my breath as I held up a photo of Harrison and someone else. The resemblance between the two men was clear. "Stevie, do you know who this is?"

Stevie squinted and stared at the photo. "No...Oh, wait a minute. He does look familiar."

"That's Indie Wilkes," I replied. "He's the guy George fired when he came back from the dead."

"Oh, yeah," Stevie said. "Whatever happened to that guy?"

"Nothing." I gulped. "I think he got his revenge in the end."

Yogi barked, and I looked up as Harrison waltzed into his office and shut the door behind him. As I held the photograph, the resemblance was clear. Harrison and Indie Wilkes, Mrs. Carmichael's former business partner, looked alike. They both had the same shade of light brown hair, and they were both short with a penchant for khaki suits.

"That is a heavy accusation." The bolt on the office door clicked as Harrison locked us in.

"Ember, what's going on?" Stevie's eyes darted around the room, and Yogi stood his ground in between us and Mr. H.

"This wasn't about a love affair or a bunch of angry mobsters George owed money to," I explained. My heart felt like it might leap out of my chest. "It's about the hotel. *He* murdered George because he wanted the hotel."

"Impressive." Harrison clapped his hands. "I had no idea you country folk were so bright. But you two can't prove a thing."

"I'm sure I can prove you're related to Indie Wilkes."

"He's my nephew," Harrison admitted. "The two of us were weeks away from taking over the hotel before George decided to show up again. Elizabeth had failed to tell me that his death had all been a lie. Of course, that killed her contract with Indie. But *I* still had a chance."

"So, you murdered a guy over a hotel?" Stevie placed her hands on her hips, not quite as alarmed as I was that Harrison had discovered us.

Harrison chuckled, and immediately I saw a glint of wildfire in his eyes.

"This isn't just a hotel, my dear. It's a legacy. There are more than just secret passageways hidden in these walls. You have no idea what this place is worth."

"And you thought the Carmichaels would just hand you their half?" Stevie argued.

"Elizabeth will see things my way," he insisted. "I'll make sure of that."

"No." I gulped, shaking my head. "There are too many loose ends for you to get away with this. For starters, there's Cindy. The police will look into her story, you know."

"Yes, I suppose I have you to thank for that one. Your picture was in the paper at the scene of that explosion at the playhouse." He sneered as his hands casually moved to his pockets.

"It was you who was trying to kill her," I stated.

"She was supposed to be on that float." He rolled his eyes. "She was late."

"How did you know about the affair?" I asked.

"Or the cheesecake?" Stevie blurted out. From the tone of her voice, I guessed she wasn't as worried as I was that Harrison had decided to spill his deepest darkest secrets.

There was only one reason he'd admitted to murder at all.

He planned on killing us too.

"I've been planning on taking this hotel for years. Naturally, I hired someone to do some digging, and I figured it out. That little tramp always brought dessert. The maids take out the trash, and they'll tell you anything for the right price. The rest was child's play. George got his usual coffee delivery, spiked with a little something extra, and then I went into the room to make sure he was dead."

"And then you waited and set up the scene," I finished.

"And with protestors storming the lobby, no one suspected a thing," Stevie added. "You're disgusting."

"That doesn't matter." Harrison pulled something out of his pocket.

I cringed as he showed me a tiny button.

"What's that?" Stevie was still in denial.

"You two will follow my instructions to the letter," Harrison said. "Otherwise, I'll push this button."

"Seriously?" Stevie argued. "I mean, it's a *button*."

"A button that will blow up your family bakery," he stated with a smirk. "Years of happy family memories down the drain. Is that what you want?"

Yogi growled and bared his teeth.

"You're bluffing." Stevie's voice quivered. She was catching on. No one in their right mind went out of their way to do what Harrison had done. He and his nephew were both insane. They were ruthless, and Harrison had blown stuff up before. Part of me believed him.

"Quiet, Stevie." I took a deep breath. "What do you want from us?"

"I want you both to follow me to the roof."

Chapter 25

Harrison didn't explain what he planned on doing.

He didn't have to.

Stevie and I followed him through hallway after hallway, and I knew where we were headed. He was taking us up to the fourth floor, where he would undoubtedly get us to jump so he could tell the police we'd been guilty after all. There was no way we could let him push that button. We had no idea who was at the bakery. Mom had a key, and Aqua used the café to study once in a while.

Testing Harrison's claims wasn't worth the risk.

As soon as we left the employees' hallway and entered the main hotel, Yogi sprinted off toward the lobby. Stevie moved to follow him, but Harrison cleared his throat. He pointed to his pocket, which housed the tiny little button powerful enough to destroy everything we owned in seconds.

"No funny business, or your bakery gets it," Harrison whispered.

He tilted his head in another direction, and Stevie and I followed him to the private elevator leading upstairs. I eyed the ceiling before stepping inside. If the police were able to get to the security cameras before Harrison, surely they would discover the truth. But Stevie and I would already be dead at that point and the recordings most likely tampered with.

After a silent elevator ride, the bell dinged, and we stepped into the Carmichaels' private lobby. Harrison led us into Mrs. Carmichael's suite, which had the largest balcony of all. Harrison locked the door and opened the French doors with a smug look on his face.

"Well, what are you waiting for?" He tilted his head toward the sea as an ocean breeze blew through the air.

"You want us to climb onto the roof?" Stevie wrinkled her nose.

Harrison immediately pulled out the detonator. "Need I remind you what's at stake here?"

"Do you expect us to jump?" Stevie argued.

"My dear, I can make life very difficult for you," he responded. "I'll start by turning your bakery into ash, and then I'll make sure you can *never* afford to rebuild it."

"Over my dead body," Stevie said under her breath.

Stevie walked toward him, but she didn't walk with caution. She didn't cower, and she didn't keep her eyes on the sheer fabric draping the patio doors and fluttering in the midday breeze. She kept her eyes on Harrison, her fists clenched tight.

She was going for it.

"Stevie, wait!" My words had little effect on her as she walked right up to Harrison and drove her fist into his face. I cringed even though the punch hadn't been for me. The sound of flesh against flesh was enough to make my skin crawl.

Harrison, strong for his size, hit her back. It was enough to knock her to the ground. My chest pounded as Stevie turned and attempted to crawl away from him. He kicked her in the stomach, and Stevie let out a gasp of air. He'd struck through to her lungs.

Horrified by what I was seeing, I ran at Harrison next.

But he was ready for me—his expression cold and his arms guarding his face.

I had no experience fighting, but I did know that when in doubt I had to aim for places that counted the most. In Harrison's case, that meant I needed to hit him with a low blow.

Literally.

Harrison grabbed my arms as soon as I was close enough, but he had no control of my knees. I struck him in between his legs and dodged out of the way as his head immediately fell forward. He yelped in pain, and the thrill of a job well done burst through my veins like a shot of adrenaline.

Stevie forced herself to stand up. She was in pain. I saw it on her face. But she walked right up to Harrison—hitting his left knee as hard as she could with the sole of her shoe. And then she hit it again. And again. And again.

Harrison screamed and fell to the floor, crawling toward the exit but failing to gain any momentum.

A loud bang echoed through the bedroom, and Yogi came running in with another furry companion. A wolf with dark, matted fur and fangs the size of an alligator's circled his prey. That prey had already been hunted.

Yogi barked at the wolf.

"Thanks for putting that secret passageway to good use, but you're too late, Thad," Stevie said loudly as she clutched her chest. "We already got him." She muttered a few curse words in Harrison's direction.

"But it's the thought that counts," I added.

Yogi barked, and Thad, still in wolf form, growled.

I turned toward Harrison as he clawed at the floor, wincing in pain. It was easy to grab the detonator. He was too distracted by his knee as he tried again to move toward the door. Thad and Yogi blocked his path, and a glint of terror flashed in Harrison's eyes as he made eye contact with the two growling beasts in the room.

"All of you will regret this," Harrison shouted. As soon as he'd uttered his threat, his eyes drooped. He went in and out of consciousness until, finally, his body fell motionless to the floor. Thad and Yogi began sniffing him.

"I think I shattered his kneecap," Stevie said. "At least, that's what I was going for."

"What made you go for the left one?"

"Oh, it's already injured," Stevie explained. "He had surgery on it several times."

"Who told you that?"

"His ex-wife's ghost." Stevie pointed at a loveseat across the room. "She's right over there, and she hates his guts."

Chapter 26

"Put that over there," Stevie instructed. "The cupcakes go over there, and make sure those cookie plates stay full."

A week had passed, Cindy had been released, and Harrison had been arrested. An article in the *Misty Messenger* had confirmed that Harrison was related to the Carmichaels' former business associate, Indie Wilkes, and a nurse at the hospital where Harrison was being treated had leaked that he'd seriously injured his knee.

That article was framed in Stevie's bedroom.

The most exciting news of all was that the Lunar Bakery was back in business. Stevie had been baking for days, and she'd even invited a few of the locals around for a grand reopening celebration. I felt like I was attending a wedding reception.

"Thank y'all for keeping us in business all of these years," my mom announced from the register. She held up her coffee cup. "Here's to more years and even more cakes."

The café was filled with neighbors and friends, both human and magical. Stevie circulated the room, holding a cake box she'd reserved just for Zinny Pellman—a sugar-free spread that needed taste testing. Yogi tagged along behind her, followed by Whiskers, who had healed enough to walk and had a newfound mission to cling to Yogi wherever he went. It had given me a nice break.

In the corner of the café was Nova. She sat at a table all alone, smiling at every onlooker and turning her nose away from the food. I approached her with caution. Our last meeting hadn't been the best, and Stevie's comment about the Siamese cat had stung.

"You came," I said, sitting in the chair across from her. Her auburn hair was in a tight bun, and her charm bracelet jingled as she rested her hands beneath her chin.

"Of course. I'm your regional representative," she replied. "It's my job to keep an eye your family."

"So, you're spying?"

"I don't see it that way." She smiled, showing off plum lipstick that went with her violet purse.

"I'm sorry about what Stevie said," I told her. "She didn't mean to offend you." I glanced over at Stevie, who had made her way to Darlene and a few of the ladies from her secret gambling club. No doubt she was fishing for an invitation by offering them free slices of cake.

"I know." Nova glanced down at the table. She cleared her throat. "You know, my grandmother had a Siamese cat that followed her around everywhere."

"I see."

"My sister used to tease me," Nova continued. "She said she would always be stuck to me just like grandma's Siamese cat." She exhaled and snuck a glimpse out the window. "I lost her in a car accident a long time ago. I guess hearing about the cat and everything brought back a lot of those painful memories."

"But she kept her promise, right?" I didn't know if I was being helpful or hurtful. "She's still around."

"Yeah." Nova sniffled and then quickly composed herself. "Yeah, she is."

"Mind if I steal her away?" A voice came over my shoulder and the muscles in my torso tensed.

"Go right ahead." Nova stood, clutching the strap of her violet handbag. "Ember deserves a little fun before I dump another case on her. Also, those key lime bars over there are calling my name."

I turned around and saw Thad. The two of us hadn't brought up our kiss at the hotel, and I didn't know if he'd planned on bringing it up at all. I tucked a strand of hair behind my ear. Aqua had curled it for me and convinced me to wear it down. But I'd drawn the line at pink and purple color streaks.

"Well, we survived Mardi Gras," I said.

"And?" He leaned in closer, studying every curve of my face.

"And I turned down that job in New York," I confessed. "Misty Key is where I'm meant to be. For now, anyway."

"That'll make this easier then."

"What?" My heart rate soared, and I hoped Thad couldn't sense it.

"Asking you out," he answered. "I hate planes. You know—wild beast in a cage."

I lightly hit his chest.

"Always the teaser."

"I'm serious this time." His thick hand touched my shoulder. "One date. You can pencil that in, can't you?"

"Possibly." I bit the corner of my lip, and my eyes darted to his. Our kiss was fresh in my mind, and I wondered if it was on his mind too.

The chatter in the café fell silent as the front doors swung open and let in a warm breeze. Mrs. Carmichael entered the bakery wearing a white skirt suit and oversized sunglasses. Stevie looked stunned, as did every other customer within sight.

"Mrs. Carmichael." I approached her slowly.

She took off her sunglasses. "I told you to call me Elizabeth."

"Yes, I remember," I responded. "What can I do for you, Elizabeth?"

The rest of the room watched her in silence.

"I just wanted to thank you and your family for what you did," Elizabeth said loud enough for everyone to hear her. "That sad excuse for a man would have slithered around my hotel for who knows how long if it wasn't for you."

"All in a day's work," Stevie chimed in.

Elizabeth didn't smile.

"Coffee and a slice of cake, please," she stated with a serious expression. Her eyes quickly widened, and her lips formed a mischievous smile. She held out her arms. "Coffee and cake for everyone. It's on me."

Stevie breathed a sigh of relief, and the rest of the room clapped and cheered.

Elizabeth Carmichael had descended from her throne at the top of the hill.

And she'd turned out to be a normal person.

"The police dropped this off." Aqua entered my office with another box.

"That better be Stevie's favorite whisk, because she swears someone at the station took it home," I replied.

The bakery had been up and running for weeks, and a few items that had been hauled off to the police station for testing were still missing. I opened the box and found a small package sitting on top of a pile of papers the police had taken out of my desk drawers.

"Hey, Stevie," Aqua shouted.

Stevie jogged into my office before I could hide it. Her eyes went wide as she stared at the package that Warner Grant had sent her. It had been opened by the police and then taped back up again. I eagerly watched as Stevie picked it up and searched for the nearest trash can.

"You're not even going to open it?" Aqua grabbed the box and began tearing at the seams.

"Aqua, stop that!" Stevie snatched the package from her.

"She's kind of right," I commented. "What's the harm in opening it? You've got to face your fears sometime, right?"

"I'm not afraid of Warner Grant," she scoffed, brushing a strand of hair away from her eyes.

"Prove it." Aqua crossed her arms and glared at Stevie.

Yogi stretched, getting up from his usual morning nap under my desk, and joined the conversation. He was followed by Whiskers. Whiskers jumped into my lap as Stevie half-heartedly opened the package.

She pulled out a letter.

"What's this?" Aqua grabbed a plastic container that had been taped shut. She struggled to open it.

"'I hope this makes up for what happened to...'" Stevie stopped reading aloud. She gulped, her eyes glossy, and skipped ahead to the end of Warner's message. "'Phoenix powder is very rare, and it has the ability to restore things to their original form.'"

"Ouch!" Aqua shook her finger as the edge of the plastic container opened and pricked her pinky.

The phoenix powder spilled into my lap.

I jumped out of my chair just as a soft orange glow surrounded Whiskers.

He slowly grew until he matched me in height.

His feline face morphed into a man's with a rounded nose.

His paws turned into human hands.

And his body was as bare as could be.

Stevie gasped.

Aqua pulled out her phone.

And I shielded my face even though the man standing in front of me didn't seem to care that he was standing completely nude in a bakery with three women.

The man stretched his arms, and his face beamed with joy.

"I thought I would never see these hands again," he stated, studying his fingers and wrists. The same scar he'd had as a cat was present on one of his palms.

"Uh, *who* are you?" Stevie asked.

"Ike," the man responded. His accent suggested he wasn't from the Gulf Coast—maybe not even the southern United States. He reached for Stevie's hand and shook it excessively. "Thank you. Thank all of you. I've been a cat for more than one hundred years."

"Are you serious?" Aqua held up her phone, but I pushed it away.

"Any reason why, Ike?" I asked.

"Oh, a witch's curse," he casually answered. "A witch from a little town in the Rockies where I used to live. Bison Creek. I doubt it's even there anymore. Anyway, I've been hanging around magical family after magical family hoping someone might figure it out and find a way to change me back. When I heard that Stevie could see the dead, I thought maybe an ancestor of mine would find her eventually. All of my family is long gone. I watched them grow old."

"I have a million questions." Aqua bounced up and down excitedly.

"Oh, I don't doubt that, Miss Aqua," Ike responded. "But first things first."

Ike stared at Stevie.

"What?" She shrugged in response.

"I heard you ladies need a baking assistant."

Red Velvet Cheesecake
Deadly delicious

Cake:
2 cups all-purpose flour
1 cup sugar
2 1/2 tablespoons cocoa powder
1 teaspoon salt
1 1/2 teaspoons baking soda
2 eggs
1 cup oil
1 cup buttermilk
2 teaspoons vanilla extract
2 teaspoons white vinegar
1 ounce red food coloring

Cheesecake:
3 (8 ounce) packages cream cheese, softened
1/3 cup sour cream
1 cup sugar
1 tablespoon all-purpose flour
3 eggs
1 teaspoon vanilla extract

Frosting:
1/2 cup unsalted butter, softened
1 (8 ounce) package cream cheese, softened
1 teaspoon vanilla extract
5-6 cups powdered sugar

Instructions

For the cake layers, whisk together the flour, sugar, cocoa powder, and salt. Add the eggs, oil, buttermilk, vanilla extract, and thoroughly combine. In a separate bowl, combine the baking soda and vinegar. After a reaction takes place, add to the batter and mix. Add in the red food coloring. Mix batter until it is the desired shade of red. Pour batter into two greased 9 inch cake pans and bake at 350 degrees Fahrenheit for 30 – 35 minutes. Cover and refrigerate.

For the cheesecake layer, use a mixer to whip cream cheese, sour cream, sugar, flour, eggs, and vanilla extract until smooth. Line the bottom of a 9 inch Springform cheesecake pan with parchment paper. Pour mixture into pan and place pan in a water bath. Bake the cheesecake at 375 degrees Fahrenheit for 45 minutes. Turn the oven off, slightly open the oven door, and leave the cheesecake in the oven for an additional 30 minutes. Refrigerate overnight or place in freezer for two hours.

For the frosting, use a mixer to whip the softened butter and cream cheese. Add the vanilla extract. Mix until thoroughly combined. Add the powdered sugar one cup at a time.

After the cheesecake has cooled, assemble cake layers by placing the cheesecake filling in between the two red velvet cakes. Fill in any gaps around the sides with frosting. Refrigerate for at least twenty minutes. Frost again, completely covering the cake. Refrigerate before serving.

Enjoy!

Acknowledgements

A special thanks to the friendly folks of Montgomery, Alabama. You know who you are. Thanks for your kindness and hospitality.

Thanks to my all of my taste testers who are down with eating sweets at a moment's notice.

Thanks Christine, Ashley, and Annie.

Thanks to all of my readers. I wouldn't be here without you.

Thank you grandma Ebby for passing down the writing gene. I think of you often and I'll never stop missing you.

Books by A.GARDNER

Southern Psychic Sisters Mysteries
Dead and Butter
Mississippi Blood Cake
Dead Velvet Cheesecake
Lemon Meringue Die
Chocolate Dead Pudding
Pineapple Upside Drown Cake

Bison Creek Mysteries:
Powdered Murder
Iced Spy
Frosted Bait
A Flurry of Lies
Dusted With Death

Poppy Peters Mysteries:
Southern Peach Pie And A Dead Guy
Chocolate Macaroons And A Dead Groom
Bananas Foster And A Dead Mobster
Strawberry Tartlets And A Dead Starlet
Wedding Soufflé And A Dead Valet
Gingerbread Fudge And A Holiday Grudge

Thanks, Y'all!

To be notified of sales and new releases, sign-up for my author newsletter by visiting my website www.gardnerbooks.com. Learn more about me and what I'm working on by following me on social media:

Facebook: @gardnerbooks
Instagram: @agardnerbooks
Pinterest: @agardnerbooks

Made in United States
Orlando, FL
22 March 2023

31295694R00157